TITUS AWAKES

Born in 1918, Maeve Gilmore was a painter, sculptor and writer. She married Mervyn Peake, author of the Gormenghast novels, in 1937 and they had three children. She is the author of *A World Away*, an account of her life with Peake. Anthony Burgess wrote of that book, 'it is impossible not to be moved by Maeve Gilmore's memoir . . . The moral of Gilmore's exquisite and poignant book is that life is hell, but we had better be grateful for the consolations of love and art.' Gilmore died in 1983.

Mervyn Peake (1911–1968) was a playwright, painter, poet, illustrator, short story writer, and designer of theatrical costumes, as well as a novelist. Among his many books are *Gormenghast*, *Titus Groan* and *Titus Alone*.

ALSO BY MAEVE GILMORE

Non-fiction

A World Away

Editor

Peake's Progress

MAEVE GILMORE

Titus Awakes

The Lost Book of Gormenghast

BASED ON A FRAGMENT BY
Mervyn Peake

WITH AN INTRODUCTION BY
Brian Sibley

VINTAGE BOOKS
London

3 5 7 9 10 8 6 4 2

Published by Vintage 2011

Vintage
Random House, 20 Vauxhall Bridge Road,
London SW1V 2SA

www.vintage-books.co.uk

Addresses for companies within The Random House Group Limited can be
found at: www.randomhouse.co.uk/offices.htm

The Random House Group Limited Reg. No. 954009

A CIP catalogue record for this book
is available from the British Library

ISBN 9780099552765

The Random House Group Limited supports The Forest Stewardship Council
(FSC®), the leading international forest certification organisation. Our books
carrying the FSC label are printed on FSC® certified paper. FSC is the only
forest certification scheme endorsed by the leading environmental organisations,
including Greenpeace. Our paper procurement policy can be found at
www.randomhouse.co.uk/environment

Typeset in Comenius by Palimpsest Book Production Limited,
Falkirk, Stirlingshire
Printed and bound in Great Britain by
CPI Group (UK) Ltd, Croydon, CR0 4YY

Contents

Introduction by Brian Sibley   vii

Foreword by Maeve Gilmore   xv

1   Titus Awakes from the Snows   1

2   Titus Among the Snows   7

3   Sacrifice. Behold   13

4   Titus's Awakening   17

5   As the Spring Awakes, So Do the
Two Strangers   23

6   Awakening Is Sweet Sorrow   27

7   Living Refound   29

8   Life Can Be a Miracle   33

9   Autumn and Winter, the Pain of Both   39

10   Away from the Mountains   43

11   Titus Learns of Other Loves   49

12   Among the Rivers   55

13   They Reach the Archipelagos and Forests   63

14   Lagoons – Fires   69

15   Among the Soldiers   75

16	Still Among the Soldiers	83
17	Back at Camp	89
18	Plans of Escape	97
19	Escape	103
20	An Unexpected Meeting	113
21	An Affectionate Welcome	129
22	Titus as Model	141
23	Titus Thinks of the Past	153
24	Moments of Serenity	159
25	At Mrs Sempleton-Grove's	167
26	From Riches to Rags	177
27	Other Places, Other Work	185
28	Among the Dead Men	191
29	Intimations of Other Days	199
30	Happening in a Side Street	207
31	Under the Masks	215
32	A Sanctuary	225
33	An Unwelcome Interlude	237
34	The End of an Unwelcome Interlude	251
35	Search Without End	257

Introduction

Mervyn, Maeve and the Search without End

This introduction includes elements of the plot

I was handed, simultaneously, a generously measured gin and tonic and a typescript in a blue-grey folder, on the cover of which was written *Search Without End*, words that would eventually become the title of the final chapter to the book you are about to read.

This was over thirty years ago and Maeve Gilmore and I were sitting in what she called the 'Petit Salon', an intimate room overlooking the backgarden of No. 1 Drayton Gardens in Kensington, London – the last home she had shared with her late husband, Mervyn Peake.

Both were artists of considerable talent and Mervyn was a remarkable polymath: in addition to being a painter and an illustrator (reinterpreting classics such as *Alice's Adventures in Wonderland*, *The Rime of the Ancient Mariner*, *Treasure Island* and *Dr Jekyll and Mr Hyde* for the twentieth century) he was also a novelist, playwright and poet. As a writer, he used the rich language of the artist's palette; repeatedly describing characters and scenes in the Titus novels in terms of composition, colour, texture, light and shade.

The walls of the 'Petit Salon' were hung with paintings and drawings and, along the back of the sofa, was a troupe of knitted dolls made by Maeve that were vaguely reminiscent of Pierrot and Columbine figures, but also kindred spirits of the tall, spindle-limbed acrobatic dancers that frequented many of Mervyn's sketch-books. Here it was that, once a month, our conversation would range across a broad spectrum of subjects from books and paintings to theatre and religion, inevitably returning again and again to Mervyn's work and Maeve's devoted endeavours to secure the memory of his reputation as an artist and writer of genius.

The typescript I had just been handed was rather more personal: Maeve's *Search Without End* was to be a continuation of the epic saga recorded in Mervyn's trilogy of novels, *Titus Groan*, *Gormenghast* and *Titus Alone*. In fact, the trilogy was never conceived as such, for the author's ambitious intention had always been to compose a cycle of novels chronicling Titus' life and travels, written in a style that is frequently categorised as a hybrid of fantasy and gothic fiction, but which is unique to its author.

The first two volumes, crowded with characters of Dickensian stature, tell of the birth, childhood and adolescence of Titus Groan and his inheritance of the title of seventy-seventh Earl of Gormenghast, a vast decaying realm in the thrall of arcane, centuries-old ceremonies. The third book follows Titus as he deserts his ancestral kingdom and finds himself an alien in a strangely futuristic world governed by the clinical, dehumanising rituals of science and technology.

By the time *Titus Alone* was finally published in 1959, Mervyn's health was rapidly disintegrating due to the onslaught of the neurodegenerative illness that would eventually claim his life in 1968 at the age of fifty-seven. Although Peake had intended to write more volumes, the first of which was to be called *Titus Awakes*, it became clear that there was no hope of his ever being able to carry his vision through to completion. All that exists of *Titus Awakes* is the fragment dated July 1960, which is clearly marked at the beginning of this book. In addition, Mervyn had drawn up a list of possible subjects for chapters. Running to four-dozen, one-word categories of places and peoples, this tantalizingly enigmatic inventory included prospective episodes in which Titus would be found, for example, among the 'snows', 'mountains', 'forests', 'archipelagos' and 'soldiers'.

Maeve would later describe these jottings as 'tragic

notes . . . the gropings of a man wishing to write something surpassing anything he had already done'.
Nevertheless, these seemingly random themes provided
her with the initial inspiration. Perhaps the daunting
challenge of piecing together Mervyn's notes into a story
was, for Maeve, a vain attempt to deny the fact that the
man, like the story he had been formulating, was now
forever lost.

Begun in 1970, two years after Mervyn's death,
Maeve's continuation and eventual completion of *Search
Without End* was neatly written in sepia-ink and filled
four black exercise books. Although, at first, Maeve wrote
without thought of publication, the manuscript was
subsequently transcribed into an ongoing series of type-
scripts, such as the one I read in the late seventies, each
with its own amendments, deletions and additions. With
Maeve's death in 1983, *Search Without End* was 'lost',
eventually coming to light, more than two-and-a-half
decades later, when her granddaughter, Christian,
discovered it in an unprepossessing cardboard box in
the family attic.

Today, when sequels to classic books written by other
hands are two-a-penny, it might be thought that Maeve
had approached the task of continuing Titus' story with
confidence. In truth, the writing began as an intensely
cathartic experiment; a humble gesture of unconditional

love and – rather in the way that Mervyn had once described the craft of drawing – as a hoped-for means of holding back astonishing and fantastical ideas 'from the brink of oblivion'.

The story that unfolds in the following pages is picaresque: a series of episodic vignettes featuring a motley collection of characters. Some are broadly caricatured, such as the pretentious poet, 'I am', and his vacuous audience of aspiring literati. Others are obviously drawn, in some measure, from life – especially, one feels, Maeve's portrait of the painter, Ruth Saxon, and her struggles with life as an impecunious artist.

References to characters in the earlier books also litter the pages. There are references to Titus' family – particular his sister, Fuchsia – and to the women who previously awaked his emotions: the ill-starred foster-sister, known only as 'The Thing', and, from *Titus Alone*, the loving Juno, the icy Cheeta and the tragic girl called the Black Rose.

Titus's new encounters are almost all threatening: either to his very existence or to his passion for freedom. His refusal to commit to those who show him affection – the mountain girl who bears his child, the dog who slavishly follows him and his short-term lover, Ruth – is, however, eventually, and unexpectedly, challenged and overturned in a development that, one suspects, must have surprised the author as much as it does the reader.

As the writing slowly progressed it evolved. What had begun as an act of homage – attempting to emulate Mervyn's narrative style – was now being expressed in Maeve's own distinctive voice which had already found eloquent expression in her emotionally charged memoir, *A World Away* (1970). The final result is a highly personal quest to understand her husband's tragic descent into illness in terms of his artistic and literary brilliance.

This quest finds fulfilment in the meetings between Titus Groan and an 'artist' who unmistakably represents Mervyn. So, unexpectedly, the creator of Titus becomes a character within Titus's universe and, at the end of the novel, is the person who, in a mysteriously spiritual sense, gives purpose and meaning to Titus's existence.

These biographical episodes contain distressingly authentic details such as the description of the austere institution where Titus works as an orderly. This was inspired by the Friern Hospital (formerly known as Colney Hatch Lunatic Asylum) where Mervyn was, for a time, confined. Less painfully, the depiction of the abbey is based on Aylesford Priory, where he had earlier spent time working on *Titus Alone* before his illness claimed most of his senses. In the book, these locations appear in a reversal of the order in which they featured in Mervyn's life, almost as if Maeve were trying to turn back the clock so that, instead of relentless decline, the artist appears to be recovering, becoming a vibrant, life-embracing person once more, represented, in the novel, by the man waiting with his three children on the island jetty for Titus's arrival.

Islands are a recurring motif throughout the Titus novels, with Gormenghast castle being frequently compared to one. It is, perhaps, the sense of isolation – even captivity – that an island can engender that contributes to Titus' desire to escape. In Maeve's perspective, however, the island increasingly comes to represent for Titus the opposite of imprisonment: a refuge, a sanctuary, a safe haven from the vacant wanderings depicted in *Titus Alone*, a place where experiences and encounters can be safely circumscribed.

Although unnamed, the island described at the end of *Titus Awakes* is very specifically Sark, the smallest of the Channel Islands, where Mervyn Peake first went to live in 1933 and where he spent two formative years of his career working with the Sark Group of artists. A decade later, in 1946, following the publication of the much-acclaimed *Titus Groan*, Mervyn returned to Sark with Maeve and their two sons Sebastian and Fabian. During their time there, a daughter, Clare, was born and Mervyn wrote *Gormenghast*. Sark would also later provide the setting for his novel of magical realism, *Mr Pye*.

For Maeve, therefore, Sark – the island that becomes Titus's final destination – represented happier times, a place of healing and wholeness, a place where creator and creation could effortlessly become one. 'Life, and the love of it was paramount,' she writes of Titus's newfound understanding. 'There was no longer any tragic groping. What he understood was a lust for life.'

As a final gesture to her husband's vision, Maeve eventually relinquished her title, *Search Without End*, in favour of the one that Mervyn had planned to use, *Titus Awakes*.

The book opens with words written by Mervyn Peake as he attempted to set out with his hero on another foray into the world that lay beyond Gormenghast. Maeve Gilmore chose to end the book by quoting Titus's mother telling her departing son: 'There's not a road, not a track, but it will lead you home.'

What makes this coda so poignant is the realisation that home is not the crumbling, time-eaten towers and turrets of Gormenghast castle, but the mind and heart of the man who built it in his imagination.

Brian Sibley, 2011

Foreword

The Gormenghast Trilogy was not envisaged as a trilogy. There was to have been a fourth book in which Titus Groan, having left his own domain of his own volition for the first time, knowing that he could not return, entered a world where he was unknown, young and alone. The life he found outside the castle was indifferent to him; there were echoes from his childhood, and the flint he carried with him gave verisimilitude, if to no one else, at least to himself.

Gormenghast was not a dream. The world he encountered outside was not a dream, and the world that had been engendered by the first three books was to encompass the vastness of life. A picaresque tale that was so bloody, and so enormous in its vision, that only a man who had that boldness and that vision within his grasp could manipulate it.

I am about to try to take *Titus Alone* into that world.

The first pages will be those that were tortured into life by the man who struggled with his failing brain, and his failing hand to conjure up so enormous a task.

Maeve Gilmore, 1970

1

Titus Awakes from the Snows

Meanwhile the castle rolled. Great walls collapsed, one into another.

The colours of the tracts were horrible. The vilest green. The most hideous purple. Here the foul shimmering of rotting fungi – there a tract of books alive with mice.

In every direction great vistas opened, so that Gertrude, standing at the little window of a high room, would seem to command a world before her eyes, though her eyes were out of focus.

It had become a habit of hers to stand at this particular window, from which a world lay bare, a clowder of cats at her feet and her dark red hair full of nests.

Who else is there alive in this echoing world? And yet, for all the collapse and the decay, the castle seemed to have no ending. There were still the endless shapes and shadows, echoing the rides of stone.

While the Countess Gertrude moved about her home, it might be thought that she was in some kind of trance, so silent she was. The only sound coming from her coiled hair was the twitter of small birds.

As for the cats, they swarmed about her like froth.

One day the massive Countess standing before the little window of her bedroom lifted her matriarchal head and brought her eyes into focus. The birds fell silent and the cats froze into an arabesque.

As she approached from the west, so Prunesquallor, his head in the air, approached from the east, and as he minced he sang in a falsetto, unutterably bizarre.

'Is that you, Prunesquallor?' said the Countess, her voice travelling gruffly over the flagstones.

'Why, yes,' trilled the Doctor, breaking off in his own peculiar improvisation. 'It most assuredly is.'

'Is that you, Prunesquallor,' said the Countess.

'Who else?'

'Who else,' said her voice, travelling over the flagstones.

'Who else,' cried the Doctor. 'It assuredly is! At least I hope so,' and Prunesquallor patted himself here and there, and pinched himself to make sure of his own existence.

The Descent from Gormenghast Mountain

With every pace he drew away from Gormenghast Mountain, and from everything that belonged to his home.

That night, while Titus lay asleep in the tall barn, a nightmare held him. Sometimes as he turned in his sleep he muttered, sometimes he spoke out loud and with extraordinary strange emphasis. His dreams thronged him. They would not let him go.

It was early. The sun had not yet risen. Outside the barn the hills and the forests were hoary with cold dew, and blotched with pools of ice.

What is he doing here, the young man, 77th Earl and Lord of Gormenghast? This surely is a far cry from his home and his friends. Friends? What was left of them. As for his home, that world of fractured towers, what truth is there in its existence? What proof had he of its reality?

Sleep brought it forth in all its guises and, as he turned again, he hoisted himself on his elbow and whispered, 'Muzzlehatch, my friend, are you gone then for ever?'

The owl made no movement at the sound of his voice. Its yellow eyes stared unblinking at the sleeping intruder.

Titus fell back against the straw and immediately three creatures sidled into his brain.

3

The first, so nimble on his feet, was Swelter, that mountain of flesh, his belly trembling at every movement with an exquisite vibration. Sweat poured down his face and bulbous neck in runnels. Drowned in his moisture, his eyes swam no larger than pips.

In his hand he carried, as though a toy, a double-handed cleaver.

At his shoulder stood something that was hard to define. It was taller than Swelter, and gave forth a sense of timber and of jagged power. But it was not this that caught the senses, but the sound of knee-joints cracking.

For a moment they beamed at one another, this dire couple in a mixture of sweat and leather – and then their mutual hatred settled in again, like a foul plant or fungus. Yet they held hands, and as they moved across the arena of Titus's brain they sang to one another. Swelter in a thin fluted voice, and Flay reminiscent of a rusty key turning in a lock.

They sang of joy, with murder in their eyes. They sang of love, with bile upon their tongues.

Those tongues. Of Swelter's it is enough to say that it protruded like a carrot. Of Flay's that it was a thing of corroded metal.

What of the third character? The lurker in the shade of Swelter's belly? Its tongue was green and fiery. A shape not easily found. It was for the main part hidden by a bush of mottled hair.

This third apparition, a newcomer to Titus's brain, remained in the shadow, a diminutive character who reached no higher than Swelter's knee-joint.

While the other two danced, their hands joined, the tiny creature was content to watch them in their foul perambulations, until loosening their grip upon one another Swelter and Flay rose to full height upon their toes and struck one another simultaneously, and Titus in his dream twisted away from them.

Mervyn Peake, July 1960

2

Titus Among the Snows

Titus awoke from a haunted sleep. The uncanny light of whiteness began to permeate his brain. Snow fell silently. Its gentle falling was cruel, condemning him to continue in his solitude, and his hunger. The door of the barn could not be moved. The owl had frozen to death. It seemed to Titus that he was the only creature in the world left alive, and as the brilliant whiteness hit the barn, he saw around him the small corpses of birds and mice, food for what he knew would be his own incarceration.

Despite his hunger and the aching cold in his limbs, a warmth of love glowed in his memory: the withdrawn magnitude of his mother whom he could not love, but whose mental elegance chastened him – his dead sister Fuchsia, passionate, ugly and beautiful all at the same time, loving him to the point of pain, for herself and for him. Nannie Slagg, so petulant and so pathetic to all but herself. Dr Prunesquallor, whose wit did not hurt.

Bellgrove, his schoolmaster, trying to muster a dignity he did not possess, and then, because physical love bears with it the power to deny all other love the 'Thing' – callous, cruel, mocking and alone, done to death by a flash of lightning before fruition, but leaving Titus so vulnerable that he carried the scar for the rest of his life.

He thought back to Muzzlehatch, a man whose hurt when his animals were destroyed by science rendered a brilliant mind oblique and nulled by shock. The pain of his mental collapse and death was more than Titus could withstand. Juno he had not loved, but with what heart he had left, he wished that he had been able to. Everything she offered Titus was generous and without intent. She gave. He received, but could not return. He was a blind man who could not hear – a deaf man who could not see. A stump of a man who did not know how to use what little he had left of his human frame. And so, with the cruelty of youth, the cruelty of a man who knew that he was loved, he left her, and never gave her another thought.

Cheetah he hated, but with less virulence than the hatred he felt for Steerpike.

Titus was engulfed by loneliness. Despite his past, and the emptiness the future promised, he did not want to die, alone, in an unknown barn, surrounded by rodents which lay, almost beautiful in the translucent light, with their claws drawn up to their frozen faces so pitifully.

He searched the barn for the smallest shred of comfort; his eyes were as sharp as had been those of the dead owl, which still clung frozen to its rafter.

The wind howled and the tears of self-pity froze like intemperate glaciers on his cheeks. As he stretched, knowing that the thrushes, starlings and woodland creatures that had entered the barn before his incarceration crept closer to him, he heard a sound that was not animal. At this strange, unexpected screeching of the barn door being feebly pushed, his frozen body gave a leap and what was left of his heart pumped chilled blood through his whole being.

He was unable to lift himself, to call out, to come to the aid of whatever it was that trespassed on that silent atmosphere. He opened his mouth to whistle his presence, but nothing came from the pursed lips. He watched, mesmerised, as the barn door slowly – gratingly – with the shriek of pain and the difficulty of a cripple, slowly opened and let in the freezing snow.

The grating of the door was an echo of the chalk on the blackboard, so long ago when he was a boy at school. Another screech, and another and another, until the hideous sound was no longer bearable. Like the breaking of the waters, it was pushed with the imperative need of a baby to escape from its mother's womb, and the dark birth lay prostrate.

Titus knew that here was another human, whether male or female he could not tell. He dragged himself across the frozen dust to the shapeless lump. His hands and legs were bound with rags, his head wrapped with whatever he had been able to twist round it, and his body, bound with straw and other matter, now twice its normal size. All he knew was that he must close the door and shut out the blizzard.

If he had not known that there was another living being whose life depended on him, he might have loosened the small and dwindling grasp he had on life. With the ungainliness that comes from disease he dragged himself nearer the door and the miraculous hexagonal snowflakes and what might in normal circumstances have taken half a second, now took what felt like an hour.

To force the door shut again took reserves of his energy that were fast dwindling. He had never possessed personal vanity, only a supreme arrogance of the importance of his inheritance, which during his wanderings grew more powerful. Forsaking this birthright, Titus entered this new world of his own free will. Anyone from his past would neither have recognised him nor cared for what they saw; a neuter, covered in rags. He dragged himself across the other heap of humanity, gradually stretching his arms to push or pull at the barn door. All he could hear, through the woollen filth that covered his ears, was so muffled – it must have been from another world. Panting, he at last reached the door and lay, arms outstretched. He pulled at a cord attached to the door, but the cord was frozen and so brittle that it snapped. Tears of frustration froze on his cheeks. With one great effort Titus pulled the door closed, letting in a gust of snow.

So much effort could only have one result – exhaustion.

3

Sacrifice. Behold

Light flooded the barn. There were sounds outside. Sounds that Titus began to discern as voices, although still distant. Titus felt half-mad from a slumber so numbed by cold, the sound of bells pierced his ears.

He could not speak.

He could not make out what lay some yards away from him; was it a hummock or a being?

The bells continued to plague him, making sounds he should understand, but could not.

Through his swollen lids he saw shapes moving. Hidden behind his frozen swaddling, which was beginning to drip, he could hear again what he remembered as voices. Yet the language was not what he could understand as language. Noises – and in his mind they were like the sound a mother lulls her child to sleep with.

The sounds were still distant and the hummock rose, but not of its own volition. A huge shape stood over him. He was insulated, yet engulfed. He was in a dream and he was not in a dream. He felt a trickle of water make its way into a stomach aching for sustenance, but fearful.

If he had had words with which to think he would have said to himself: 'That is a dog, and those other shapes are men.' Without words he understood faintly what he saw, as a feeble light made its way across the carnage to where he lay, he felt his body being lifted with the gentleness of a lepidopterist pinning his captured beauty to a board, before enclosing it in its glass case.

Voices came and went like the tides; no rough seas here, but rhythmic and peaceful. He knew that such peace might never be his again. His thoughts came and went with the tides and he floated, a piece of flotsam back and forth, into voices and out again.

The cargo that had been jettisoned in his barn was gone. Now, he – Titus – was going to follow.

There was a light, not of this world: pink, rosy, gleaming, brilliant. There was still the murmur of voices.

No roughness. Sometimes a gliding, and sometimes a sliding, and the uncanny sound of a mountain horn, not a warning as that of a horn in a sea mist.

It was to occur to him, very much later, that he was the cause of danger to the intrepid men with their mountain dog, and it was only then that he could begin to think of repayment. But how?

∘ ∘ ∘ ∘ ∘

He opened his eyes and felt himself. His legs and arms were there. He could see and, as he shouted, he knew he could hear. He could make noises, and he repeated to himself the names of the people who had been his childhood, and those who had been his youth, and those who had come and gone again like ghosts in his young manhood. He called up the rooms he had known – he counted the dead. He called and called for his sister Fuchsia, and as he slowly held out his arms and found an emptiness, he knew that he was alive.

'I am awake,' he shouted. 'I am Titus Groan – where am I?'

An old woman swam into his vision. She smiled and shook her head. She pointed her finger to the further corner of the room.

He saw a shape. He thought, perhaps I cannot see, or what I see is not there. He looked again. This time there was a little more comprehension. It was the face of a woman. He called out, 'Fuchsia?'

His violet eyes sought out the shape across the room. Something came into focus, but what it was he could no longer tell. There was an echo of something familiar, but it was hidden beneath the layers of memory as delicately poised as *mille-feuilles*. He dared not enquire yet into the mystery, which lay as inert as he himself.

The return of sentience is so slow and so painful that there are those who wish to delay it, and others who wish it never to return, but Titus had, for all the pains he had endured in his own home and out of it, clung to life.

4

Titus's Awakening

A warmth of body lit up his whole spirit. His eyes opened willingly, for the first time since his incarceration in the freezing barn.

He knew himself to be in a room that was a room of poverty. His eyes searched and saw it all. There was so little to see. A rafter with a ham that brought back to him other rafters in vaster places, with a rat that had been crunched to death by a man so vile that he closed his eyes to forget.

When he opened them again, at the side of his pallet bed he saw an old woman holding a bowl to his lips, urging his mouth to open. Her eyes were red-rimmed by age, and as he opened his mouth to receive the blessing of food, she smiled and her toothless gums were sweeter at that moment than any young woman's lips. Liquid from the rough-hewn wooden bowl was gently poured down his throat by means of an equally rough spoon. Thus cared for, Titus enjoyed the sense of peace of an infant at its mother's breast, although this was something that had not been his to know. How could he remember being suckled by Keda, his wet-nurse from the 'Outer Dwellings' of Gormenghast? He could only recall the insatiable, unsatisfied love he had felt for her daughter – his own foster sister – the 'Thing', and the world of Gormenghast to which he clung, hated and loved.

As the last spoonful trickled down into his whole being, he closed his eyes and a sigh of more than physical satisfaction broke the silence of the poor room. As a blind man could sense, so did he. He knew that in this room was another being, apart from the old woman, who also needed succour. 'I must open my eyes. I must be a part of everything.'

The back of the old woman hid from view what he wished to see. He could only discern her movements. The old black-robed arm moved with the regularity of a tin soldier hitting his drum, up and down, but noiselessly. When the old woman ceased and moved from where she had been crouching, succouring another being, the light fell on two dark burning eyes, luminous as the snow had been. Eyes, huge and as yet unseeing. Titus felt such a yearning that his stomach, which had been hollow for so long, turned over, and the sickness he had hitherto known as lust he realised was some kind of love.

'Who are you? We were in the barn together. Your hair is still shaved, but your eyes are beautiful. They're burning me. Somewhere in my memory is a story of burning – but what it is I cannot remember. Perhaps I never knew, perhaps it is only a memory that never existed except in my own mind – or something that Fuchsia . . .'

Titus closed his eyes to recall the sister who could only love with her whole being, and then only a few chosen people, and of the few, her brother most of all. 'I'll never see her again – I'll never know again the ardour of a love that knows no physical desire.'

Daylight shone through the small latticed window, and it seemed as though there was nothing in the room but those two huge identical midnight pools of water, with twin half-circles of light that searched him out. The light from the pools shone with such brightness that Titus could not but be charged by them. The eyes continued their search and found his face and his eyes, so different, so knowledgeable. He wanted them to smile, and he wanted the smile to be returned. Four eyes searching.

Why was it that now, as he lay immobilised, his past returned to him in the memory of a girl called 'Black Rose'? She was a victim, and she shared the same look, the translucent skin and enormous black globes, and who, he had been told, died as her head touched the white pillow, and her emaciated body lay between virgin sheets. Titus asked himself if he would for ever only be able to see things present in terms of his own past. Would he never free himself?

Those black brilliant eyes hunted him out, concentrating on him like the sun's rays burning a piece of glass. He felt his cheeks flush, his mouth open, and a spasm of desire rendered him nearly insensible.

'My name is Titus,' he said in a cracked voice.

The eyes continued without blinking to search his face.

'I am Titus Groan.'

'I am Titus – I am Titus,' and his voice became shrill with impotence.

He pushed all the bed coverings away from him in a determination to move. He looked at himself and did not recognise what he saw. Two stick insects to support his torso, and at their furthermost end a pair of feet, white, unused and wrinkled. He threw the insects over the bed and, as his feet touched the cold stone, he fell ignominiously. There was no strength in him.

He raised his head to the eyes that were impelling him – the head raised upon an arm so thin that he knew his own incarceration was as nothing compared to what had reduced the once-rounded whiteness of flesh to the pathetic bone-covered skin he saw opposite him.

He had intended to violate that flesh. He had wanted to hurt, because of his own hurt, but his weakness forbade him, and instead of the insolent virility of young manhood, he felt his body rendered down to the feebleness of age, and he no longer cared that he was a ludicrous sight.

5

As the Spring Awakes,
So Do the Two Strangers

Sunlight, an intruder in the solitary room, rippled on the bare walls, mysterious and beautiful. Time had ceased to have meaning. The old woman who was both nurse and maid fed Titus and his companion. As the food became more solid, so Titus felt his strength returning.

He had ceased to call out his name, and had used the long hours of silence to return over and over again to his childhood, and to his more immediate past, conscious always of the dark beauty watching him. There was no communication, only silence, which he realised was no longer lonely. He learned to enjoy the quiet but his youthful spirit could not be damped down or put out like the dying embers of a fire. He longed to rejoin life, to tread the perilous path of the living.

There came a day when the old toothless woman placed in front of him food that he was to tackle himself. Like a clown, she mimed the movements of eating and as she watched his clumsy, inelegant jostling of food into his mouth, she nodded her head with pleasure. A great soft cream paw laid itself gently on his knees, and he saw what he must have heard when he was lifted out of oblivion: a huge but gentle dog. A soft, sensuous muzzle nudged his cheek, yelped a little and nestled under his chin.

I am me . . . I am alive . . . I am beginning again.

'Who are you?' he shouted, knowing that his question would remain unanswered. 'What can I do to bring life into these limbs?'

As Titus pushed back the coverings of his pallet bed, this time his two sticks felt a quiver of sentience in them. He was careful – he knew that it was only time that would bring back to him the movements he had always taken for granted.

The dog bounced excitedly, like a child filled with joy at the promise of a feast and his eyes turned expectantly on Titus.

A door was open and through it came a world from outside, a mild sun, a small breeze, a gentle tongue that licked his cheeks and his unused legs.

Oh, I want to live. I want to be alive.

Longing to stretch from foot to crown, Titus launched himself on to the stone floor and this time he did not fall. He had somewhere to go. Although his movements were that of an old man, his brain, and all his stirrings – his body and its needs – were those of a young man, deprived for too long of its necessities.

He clung to the huge dog, his arms round its neck, as it propelled him, screaming inwardly with desire, towards the bed opposite. The limping journey from pallet to pallet seemed to take an eternity.

He lay, panting, at the foot of her bed. The dog whined as Titus tried to stand, trod on its front paw and fell across the bed. 'I want you.' He lay across the tiny limbs, sighing. Frustrated tears streamed down his cheeks. 'Who are you?' Beneath the bedclothes was the faintest stirring. Was it a hand? The flutter of a butterfly traced its wings across his eyelids, down his hollow cheeks, on to his thin lips and over his chin, and stayed itself round the unshaven neck.

Adventure had begun again. He had awakened to a new life.

6

Awakening Is Sweet Sorrow

The door was wide open. Whiteness had given place to the brilliant green that presages the torrent of living. Sounds of humans: a horn, unlike the haunting alarms at sea, echoed around the mountains, sweet, deep and eloquent. Through the open door poured sunlight of such intensity that Titus was impelled to shriek, as a baby new born hails its own entrance into the world.

He saw a movement across the room – everything was awakening. He heard birdsong – he heard sounds that he could not place – muscular, masculine sounds. A saw cutting through logs – a double-edged saw – voices shouting to each other with the glory of sunshine.

He wished to be at one with those voices and his determination took him stumbling, crawling, undignified to the open door.

He gazed, as one who had been blinded, at the stupendous beauty of nature. His eyes could only take in so small a part of what there was to be seen.

He might have toppled over the mountains that surrounded him, as he drank in the air, the sky, the deep green of the trees, but for arms that held him and laid him gently on a bench, roughly hewn, and placed in his hand a mug that was lifted to his lips and, as he drank, his body and his mind were suffused with gratitude.

At his feet lay the warmth that had nestled him and nursed him through the months of cold fatigue. He glanced down and a paw, gentle and huge, laid itself upon his knee. He turned his head to the right and a thrill like a shriek of lightning coursed through his body, as he saw beside him those dark eyes devouring him.

Titus knew now that speech was no longer efficacious. He put down the mug, and found a hand, ready to take his own – a gentle, frail and blue-veined hand, which clung to his as though it had been stitched by a surgeon on to his.

All thoughts had flown. Only occasionally does human beauty so transcend all that one knows.

7

Living Refound

As the sun entered the lives of his unknown benefactors, and of himself, Titus longed to renew the grasp, so long subdued, that he held on life.

He no longer felt it necessary to assert 'I am me – I am Titus'.

The old woman, who was a part of his life now, nodded her head with pleasure at every new gesture he made, as he found his way from his bed to the door unaided, as he sang, as he twirled her gently and slowly in his arms, round and round the stone floor in a dance that brought back to her, inevitably, echoes of a long-distant youth.

The silent woman, with her huge eyes, sat still as an Eastern goddess on a bench by the open door, and when his newfound vigour expended itself her hand moved imperceptibly to take his, as he seated himself beside her.

'Is it love?' he wondered. But the need to make

recompense was uppermost now; in a practical way to repay the care given to him so generously by people to whom poverty was as much a part of living as being born and dying. The two pallet beds had been the only resting place for the tired limbs of the old woman, and the shepherds and huntsmen whose voices he had heard. The generosity of the poor knew no bounds. And now, at last, Titus knew to whom he was beholden – the faceless and the generous ones who had given, with no expectancy of return.

He forced himself outside for the first morning. The lit world nearly annihilated him, but he slid down the grass slopes longing to give of all that was within him; to thank in a physical way.

He ploughed into life, as though it was water, diving and coming up again into the air, breathing life, new and rare. He sought sounds. He traced them down a small path, hedge-lined, where small birds nested, until he came to an open space where he saw men with two-handed saws, working through, rhythmically, huge boles of trees. They were surrounded by the neat, stacked results, like intricate piles of matches, but these would not fall at a touch.

Titus joined the men. They clapped as they saw him, and he indicated by a gesture, so learned was he in mime, that he also wished to take one of the saws.

An elderly man, stained by the elements and wrinkled, stood aside, and also by a gesture indicated to Titus that he could take his place.

Everything that is mastered appears to the spectator to be easy in execution and Titus, with the ebullience of an amateur, took hold of the saw that had been given up to him. At a word, quite incomprehensible to Titus, from the man at the other end of the saw, he started to move his arms. He had seen the rhythm and the ease, and he thought that he, too, would slip into the same movements, but he was clumsy to the point of self-embarrassment, and the saw wriggled like a worm under his inexpert guidance. He felt an arm take hold of him, rather as a mother might guide her child in the use of a pencil, and with immense patience his arm was gently moved, backwards and forwards, in duet with the man at the other end, who urged Titus on.

Very gradually the rhythm came to him, but at the same time the physical exertion overwhelmed him. As he sank to the carpet of mossy grass in exhaustion he felt the strong arm that had held his behind the saw slowly change to a soft loving arm. He turned to see the two black pools enveloping him and a dew of pride overflowing down the pale cheeks.

He was ashamed of his weakness and almost roughly edged his hand away as he strove to rise again from beside the girl. His arms ached with the new-forced exertion. His body was weak and his brain angry with frustration.

He knew that he had exerted himself as much as his tired body was capable of, and he crept back to his bed, humbled, and lay with his arms over his face to shut out what he thought of as his defeat.

8

Life Can Be a Miracle

As the elements became more clement, Titus's growing strength engendered in him an awakening of all his senses. He became aware of the awe-inspiring beauty of the mountains that surrounded him, snow-laden at their tips and brilliant green as they gently swam downwards to deep fir-lined valleys. Everything around him was a miracle. The small mountain flowers, the sounds of water, birds and human voices and the mild sun overhead generated not only warmth, but also a sense of renewal in the act of living.

Titus went every day to the clearing and each day he became a little more expert at manipulating the double-handed saw. There was no verbal communication, just the rareness of being one with the men with whom he worked. His muscles became hard and his face lost its pallor.

Inside the hut the girl's beauty grew no less haunted, but it had the recognition of love in it. She had taken it upon herself to relieve the old woman of the harder household tasks. When there was a rabbit to be skinned, she would seat herself at the bare scrubbed table and skin it. No one knew what feelings she may have had in undertaking this macabre task. Chickens and birds of many varieties she plucked, with knowledge gained from her old mentor, and she took the task of cooking upon herself.

When the weather was mild enough the food was brought outside. Home-made bread was dipped in the stews and the wooden plates wiped clean with it. Each meal was received with the graceful acknowledgements of hand-clapping, and sometimes one of the men would sing, melancholy and haunting, or a man and a woman would dance with slow, intricate steps, their bodies hardly moving, while the watchers moved their hands like sighs.

A man with a musical instrument, made by himself during the long and dark winter, jumped into the circle like a jack-in-the-box, and as he played, a round of girls and boys, and men and women, danced with primitive pleasure.

Titus realised that it was also for him to contribute. He felt untalented. He could not sing, play an instrument or even dance. With a quick jump he entered the circle, and the cream-coloured dog who had attached itself to him followed him like a shadow.

He held it upright on its hind legs, and to the bizarre music of the old musician he danced round and round and round, like a top spinning, until he was so dizzy that he lost all sense of balance and fell with little grace on to the moss, and his canine friend lay panting beside him.

The applause that greeted him echoed down the mountains, and he rose and bowed with a clown-like foolishness, and led his canine partner, and stood it on its hind legs once more, and bowed its head so deep that it almost lost its dignity.

Titus bowed again and, with the humour he had for so long forgotten to be a part of his life, waddled out of the circus, his feet forming one straight line holding the right paw of his cream-furry friend who sped like a startled willow warbler.

The days followed each other in the wonderment of spring and inevitably to a young man this wonderment of nature could not contain itself in looking alone. In Titus, also, the sap rose, and the pangs of desire led him to the girl with whom he could hold no communication. He wanted more.

In the beauty of these spring evenings he led her to a small clearing he had discovered, surrounded by black-thorn in which there were nests woven as though by a master craftsman. All around them the newborn rabbits scuffled and darted about. There, on the moss, he made love to her and those eyes that still devoured him. Was it love or the physical necessity that impelled him almost to desecrate a body? Her body was compliant, yet seemed to have known a suffering to which Titus shut his eyes.

As spring gave way to summer, her emaciated body became fuller and carried within it his child. He realised he had no wish to spend his life with this woman, but he knew that what little decency he had should wait its term.

Titus threw himself into all the work that surrounded him, the planting and the sowing, the weeding, and all the preparations made by humans to stave off the winter ahead, when they live in a world dependent on their own skill and their own labour.

He had long since returned the pallet bed to the old woman, and slept where and when he could.

The dark eyes became more painful to watch, as the months proceeded and, as he acknowledged within himself his own infidelity, he wished to hide from them, and from her, more and more. He knew that she realised her burden was hers to face alone. He would leave her, but when she didn't know. He made love to her still, but he felt less and less urgency. He had not wished to propagate and the very fact that he had done so lessened his desire for her.

He detected a cooling of the friendship he had made with his fellow men, as the woman grew. Any tenderness he felt for her turned to an aggrieved sense that he was trapped. If he had had any feeling for her, perhaps he would have had the empathy to realise that she was trapped too, far more than he.

The surrounding mountains now made him claustrophobic and in his cowardice he worked out how he might escape when the time was appropriate.

The seasons were never so slow in passing from one to another. The spring that had brought about his newfound liberation took aeons in giving way to summer. He longed for his freedom. No longer did his companions clap his existence. He felt an outcast. It was as though everyone was waiting for him to go, and the eyes most of all.

9

Autumn and Winter, the Pain of Both

Darkness came earlier now. The leaves were piled into mounds and the smell of autumn twisted high into the sky, coiling with the wind. The evenings were empty of activity and potent with unease. The skies were laden, and as the body grew more full, Titus could think only of Fuchsia. Over and over again he called to the girl, pointing to her stomach, 'Fuchsia – Fuchsia.'

The only being that still clung to Titus was the cream-coloured dog. It followed him and sat at his feet as the evenings grew cold, portending winter. The logs, sawn in the days when he was learning to live again, fuelled the fire in the small room and conjured up magical warmth.

Expectation smothered him. He knew he was vile, but he did not know how to combat it. He felt that if he could speak and be understood, perhaps he could make a case for himself, yet at the same time he knew that he had no case to make. He would leave the eyes, as he had left one after the other of the people who could have loved him, but echoing always in his mind and body was the one who would continue to haunt him throughout his life – the 'Thing', loveless, heartless, cunning and cruel.

The days and nights were interminable. If he could have found the courage within himself, Titus would have torn himself free and rushed down the mountains and away. But his fate was sealed, as was that of the girl who had given him everything that a woman can give and asked nothing in return, except to await the advent of his child.

The days were still spent in physical labour and, as they shortened, Titus felt surrounded by a steadily growing animosity. He spoke only to himself. He heard the voices calling to each other and he was not of them. There was nothing to do any more but wait, and the waiting was hard to bear. Mist covered the mountains and clouded his brain. By his inexpert calculation and the slowing of the woman's movements, there would be two more months to wait. If Titus had been able to feel concern for anyone but himself, he would have known how much his tenderness was needed. She craved affection and found it in the old woman and the others in this little mountain home.

The snow began to fall once more and he was awoken

one night by the soft moaning of pain. The old woman, knowledgeable in childbirth, moved deftly out of her bed and across the room at a speed surprising in one so old.

His child was making an early entrance to a bitter world. Titus left the two women inside, and he and the dog walked round the impoverished hut. As the whiteness fell around them his child was born. The dog whimpered, then let out a howl, which coincided with the scream of the baby released from its mother's womb. The scream subsided into unholy silence.

Titus entered the hut, and looked at the mother on the bed. She knew now the years of emptiness that lay ahead of her, as tears chased each other down her pale cheeks. She held out her frail arms and murmured the only words that had ever passed between them, 'Fuchsia, Titus,' then turned away.

Titus's heart was as cold as the infant on the bed, as he made his way out of the hut.

10

Away from the Mountains

As he left the hut he heard breathing behind him – it was a mixture of the dog, and the hiss of hatred from the men and women with whom he had lived for nearly a year.

Knowing he would leave when the time was ready, he had concealed a little way down the mountain provisions that would go some way to relieve his hunger pangs. He had not anticipated having a companion, so he would have to ration the supplies, but to think of another winter like the last one was anathema to him.

It was dusk as he made his way down the path to the clearing where his child had been conceived. He put all feelings of conscience behind him. His life lay ahead. He now knew that any permanent relationship was not for him. His desires would be peremptorily fulfilled and he would hide consciousness of the pain he might inflict deep in the well of his mind.

With the provisions he had hidden a skin that would

not be missed. They were buried in the earth so that the weather could not touch them. As the snow fell, he was glad of his secret precautions. Now, after a year hemmed in by the mountains, he longed for the sight and the sound of water. His objective was to reach a sea and the mysterious outline of islands, whether inhabited or not. He yearned to see those porpoise-shaped islands emerging from the sea mist. His youth urged him on to conquest. He knew himself to be selfish, to have turned his back on the people who cried to him for help. He lived only for himself. He thought back to his other worlds, where he had cared, and been cared for, and given his strength to kill the most heinous of villains – Steerpike – and the man from the Under River.

'I am not wholly despicable,' he said out loud to himself and to the dog who warmed his freezing body. 'Perhaps one day I may prove again that I am not wholly selfish – where and when will it be?'

The dog opened its jaws and howled in sympathy.

As the day broke, they nursed their frozen limbs, and saw through the mist the pale pink path Titus knew would lead him to a sea. They broke the sullen bread and scooped the frozen snow for sustenance before they left the hollow and began to make their way. Titus followed the unworn path through thorn bushes, hearing the frightened screeches of birds. On the ground a grass snake twisted, curving away from him like a femme fatale.

'You beast, you are alone, with a man who is searching, but I don't know for what I am searching. I have forsaken love, companionship, community. And you, faithful beast, you are alone and, when the time comes, I will forsake you too. Why so pitiless?'

His words echoed up and down the mountains, as he and the dog were scourged by icy wind. 'I was not always selfish. I loved Fuchsia. I loved Dr Prune – I loved Bellgrove. I revered but feared my mother. But I was only at one with the "Thing", who was nothing but a dream, appearing and disappearing, and then gone for ever, and the man who wore faithfulness like a garment, alone like me, in the woods of Gormenghast. What was his name . . . ?'

Titus pulled at brambles, pushing aside overhanging bushes. 'What was his name? May? Day? Clay? Hay? Say? Jay? Pray – pray, pray – oh, Mr Flay – yes, Mr Flay with the creaking knee-joints. How you would despise me. Titus the traitor – but also a traitor to himself. And now I want to live, as I have never lived before. I want to see everything this new world has to offer me.'

Titus relished the freedom that was his – not looking further ahead than the next step. As he rounded a corner in the downward path he spied a hut, built from hacked-down trees, primitive but inviting. He sang and he ran. The dog bounded joyfully beside him.

The signs of a human activity hung outside the hut. Animal skins stretched pathetically, their lives stripped from them. Small flowers clung to life as the winter advanced.

He could not pass the hut without his curiosity being assuaged – he called out 'Hello' in every pitch of voice he could manage, from the deep bassoon to the shrill shriek of a cockatoo. From inside the hut he heard movements and he smelled the richness of some animal cooking. The door of the hut was suddenly opened.

What Titus saw was not what he expected. He had thought to see a figure unkempt and old, a shadow, but he saw a youngish man, in clothes that were particularly clean with the well-washed, scrubbed paleness of sun and water. The man had shoulder-length hair, beard, moustache; he was hirsute but immaculate.

At the door to his hut he bowed to Titus with the delicacy of one who had lived in another world. He bade him enter, and with added grace bowed to Titus's companion, the titanic canine. Titus had expected confusion. He had expected distaste for a stranger, but what he saw was something of infinite charm. A room, whitewashed and rich in what it had to offer. Sitting cross-legged on a floor covered by reed matting was a girl.

Then she stood as eminently as any hostess in a palace holding in her arms a baby, with the same flaxen hair that was hers. The baby cried at the sight of his dog. Titus felt ungainly and ugly, but he took the girl's hand and kissed it with a courtesy that he had long since forsaken. There was no awkward silence. The warmth of fulfilled love permeated the hut.

'I am Titus, 77th Earl of Gormenghast,' he said, 'and this is the companion of my wanderings.'

'I am Elystan and this is my wife Meirag, and this is my son, John Donne.'

The child was put down on the floor, and it crawled across the room to where the giant dog lay, with its tail hitting rhythmically the rush matting. It made no move as the infant came nearer, but looked on curiously. Titus was frightened as the little creature put its hand out to caress, but he need not have been, as the huge tongue emerged from its cream-furry mouth, and licked the baby's hand, then its face, and the mutual delight cast all fear from the adults.

11

Titus Learns of Other Loves

As the mist descended on the hut, so did tranquillity on the home in which he found himself. Oil lamps were kindled and a log fire glowed, and a harmony he knew would never be his suffused Titus until he slept beside the sleeping child and his dog and his desire to be at one with nothingness.

When he awoke it was to the sound of a flute, mellow, melancholy and sweet. Tears, which he had thought gone for ever, flooded his eyes. Elystan was playing what Titus was later to discover was a recorder, which he had made himself and which he held vertically in front of him as he played, both hands making games on the candlelit white-washed walls. He played simple music, all that the instrument allowed, and he heard another voice, that of the girl who sang in harmony, almost as a second instrument.

Mutual happiness and love are together so rare that Titus lay quietly savouring it at second hand, wishing it could last, and holding it in his mind, so that when the ugliness of life usurped this beauty he would see it ever after as a miniature, something to be carried with care into the unknown worlds that lay ahead of him.

Both the man and the girl became aware that he was awake, and their music ended.

'Well, Titus, did you sleep the sleep of the just, like your faithful hound?'

'I slept, but I cannot say if justice is the word I would use. It was mercifully blank until I became aware of the music of the gods. Perhaps that was their justice. I awoke in heaven and it looks as though I am still there.'

'We must fall short of heaven,' said Meirag. 'You must be hungry, Titus. We have been waiting for you to wake, before we do anything so mundane as eating.'

Titus sprang up, eager to taste the delights with which the rough-hewn table was laden.

Titus wished to make recompense – he wanted to thank his hostess and his host, and without warning he chanted:

How fly the birds of heaven save by their wings?
How tread the stags, those huge and hairy Kings
Save by their feet? How do the fishes turn
In the wet pinkness where the mermaids yearn
Save by their tails? How does the plantain sprout
Save by that root it cannot do without?

'This is my contribution. A nonsense rhyme from one whom I knew long ago, in another world. The verses belong to a dead man, silent in his grave, but those are his words and I offer them to you, as a thanksgiving for the shelter, the warmth, the love that is generated here. One day, when I am alone again, I will talk of your kindness to people whom I have yet to meet.'

The baby was put to bed in a cot made of clay and covered by the fleece of lambs. 'Titus,' said Elystan, 'let's eat now, and then tell us your story, a story as yet without an end.'

Titus took his place at the table to eat the flesh of the animal whose stretched skin he had noticed outside the hut. 'Oh, this is good food and cooked so well.'

The wife, with an intuition sometimes common to women, placed her hand on Titus's, at the same time looking at her husband. 'Come now, Titus, tell us your story. We will believe it, and remember it, when you have gone. Let's go by the fire.'

Titus, with the cream dog at his knee, began his tale. He spoke for hours, until the fire no longer lit his face or those of his listeners. Names and memories emerged from the mist of time – Gertrude, Sepulchrave, Fuchsia, Juno, Cheetah. Was it fairy tale? Was it truth?

'Titus, it is too much. I am overwhelmed. I know that

you, truth or no truth, can never be a part of any world but your own,' said Meirag.

'I must not live in the past,' he cried, 'but how else can I live? I can never stand still again. This is your present and your future, and your past. I envy you.'

The fire no longer sent shadows on to the walls. The quiet was broken by the tiny tap of branches on the window. Titus could see in the half-light the man and woman, arms and bodies so closely locked that they made but one shadow. His hand felt a warmth, not of human flesh, but of canine fur, beside him.

'It is time for us to go, my friend.'

So Titus lifted himself, as silently as he could so as not to disturb his new friends. The girl almost in her sleep pointed to a package on the table. Food, that only and most valuable possession of a wanderer, was there, with a note, which said, 'Goodbye, Titus. We will always remember you.'

'I will always be a traitor. Dog, dog, stay here, where you will be warm and fed.' He stumbled, feeling like a blind man his way to the table. He could not do without food, but he could do without his dog. With the food were placed garments of such warmth that he knew only a woman would think of it. He made his way to the door of the hut and, opening it so that the cold should not enter, he closed it upon the sleeping figures and the dog.

Titus heard the pitiful whines, the scratching at the door, the torment of being left behind, and before his conscience could decide what it should do he heard the latch open and close, and the panting of the creature who wished to share his exile. As Titus stumbled towards the sound of water, he turned and saw at the window a pair of eyes, and a hand raised in farewell.

12

Among the Rivers

Linger now with me, my only
On the far and distant shores,
Lingering can be so lonely
When one lingers on one's own.

'Dog, we are destined to be lonely. We are destined for the far and distant shores. You had a small choice and you made it, and now you are here. We have only one way to go. Down, and down and down towards the water, through the snow, meeting whom? Howl for me, so that we know we are together alone. I am glad that you came with me, Dog, but I owe you nothing. I want to be responsible to no one, to no thing. It's all over, living and loving; breathing is all that is left.

As day broke Titus ran and Dog bounded, sometimes before, sometimes behind – stopping to nuzzle deep into a lair, hidden to all eyes but those of the animal world. Excited by the scent of prey, Dog rushed here and there and everywhere, returning at all times to Titus. A fitful sun emerged, only to taunt and disappear, and a blinding storm of snow covered them until they were a snowman and a snow dog, running for their lives. Titus's cheeks were red as holly berries, dripping with ice, and he was glad of the warm clothes given to him. They heard a gentle trickle of water and, like the water, they ran, ignorant of the direction that they were taking, only that they were plunging seawards.

There were the last frugal remnants of food, stale crusts, dampened and made a little more palatable by the snow.

'Dog, I can't go through all this again. Last winter I was a clown of ice and it looks as though this winter will turn us both into pillars of ice. Would it be a good deed to wring your yellow-in-snow neck, Dog? Shall I end your torment before it begins?' In answer, the dog howled with dreadful understanding. The rugs and blankets that had been so generously given were still a comfort, but food was another thing. Titus had known hunger, and was to know hunger again, but he felt he could not inflict it on another being, albeit canine. But his hands were powerless to stop the breathing, the panting, and even amid his despair he delighted in the presence of his dog.

'Let's sing, Dog.'

The sunlight falls upon the grass
It falls upon the tower
Upon my spectacles of brass
It falls with all its power
It falls on everything it can
For that is how it's made;
And it would fall on me, except,
that I am in the shade.

'Oh, Dog, we are surely in the shade. Is there such a thing as not being in the shade? But what beauty is there being in the shade?'

As Titus feverishly spoke, so did nature. A ray of lightness, of pink chill, warmed the sky and gave impetus to the running, slippery, icy foot- and padsteps.

And so the sound of water, which can be beautiful – can be petrifying, can drown, or embalm – came closer and closer to them.

Titus remembered another sound of water, and another, in his own home, when the water flooded the castle, and again, when he awoke on unknown shores and he thought his life was over. A terrible pain seared him, as he knew there was no longer home and he felt he could only abandon life, and yet his feet, sore and swollen, hedged him down and down, until he could go no further; and as a dreadful repeat of last year, he fell and lay with the yellow-in-snow dog beside him, both nearly frozen to death.

A boat picked him up. Titus was used to not understanding languages. Eyes spoke, hands spoke, bodies
spoke, but lips only opened and closed, and tongues
made sounds. Communication was made by the prowess
of the particular individual in miming his desires, his
jokes were the jokes of silent clowns and his love
unspoken, save through eyes and hands.

There were three men with stubbled chins – each
could have played the villain in some age-old ritual of
the theatre. Everything about them was vile, villainous,
and they were interchangeable, with their small mean
eyes and their coarse insensitive faces. When they pulled
Titus into their boat it was not through pity or love,
but greed; they saw the dog and the warm rugs that
covered them. Their presence evoked a dreadful fear.
Titus knew that he was not being carried to safety, but
to a different kind of battle, and he knew now that he
would have to defend his dog against the hunger so
rampant in the six eyes that were fixed on skinning his
beast, and tearing it, to feast upon its flesh. He could
see these dreadful vultures and he hoped that his wiles
would be cunning enough to circumvent them when
the time came.

Titus and his companion dog, whom he was coming
to love, lay in the boat as it made its perilous way down-
stream. There was still no shelter and the snow, so

beautiful, yet so merciless, strayed into their eyes, and little icicles hung on all the protuberances that man is heir to.

The small coracle-like boat drifted mostly, as it was swept helplessly by the torrents and the icy winds. Did those men, who had grasped them out of the edge of despair, know where they were going? Sly people do nothing without a motive and as the moments drifted and the snowflakes descended, he realised more and more that their purpose in salvaging him was his dog, and he wondered why they had not just taken the dog and left him to die. But his dog had strength and would not without a fight, bitter and vicious, have left his master.

'Now,' thought Titus, 'I am bound by love and gratitude, once more, but to an animal whose only motive is unquestioning love. Do human beings ever have that exquisite selflessness?'

Titus caught a glimpse of a small reed hut – a palace in no-man's-land. The terrible trinity were making for it and, as he glanced at the hut and then at the men, he saw that he was a captive, as the worst of the three made an obscene gesture at Titus, as of cutting his throat, and at the pale melon-coloured dog of disembowelling it and scooping out the entrails and eating them. Then the first human sound rent the air, as the frail boat shook to the disgusting laughter these gestures had engendered in their maker.

Speed was now uppermost in Titus's mind as he laid his plans in the quickly descending dusk. If his captors had had more intelligence they would have separated him from his companion, but they clung closer and closer together – man and beast both aware of their danger.

The boat pulled slowly sideways towards the hut. Who were these men? What was left of their tattered clothing indicated that they must be deserters from some unknown military or totalitarian regime. Despite their coarse exterior and their seeming bravado, there was a sense of unease, of fear in their behaviour, which communicated itself to Titus. He knew they would be rash, harsh and inhuman, and this made his own plans craftier, his thoughts more secretive and his responses to them more obsequious. Dusk would be his advantage.

The coracle drew slowly towards the bank, and towards the hut, and towards a stake where countless travellers had moored their boats. Not for any of these travellers was the wonder at the end of a voyage where people gathered to welcome, only darkness and bitter cold greeted them.

A sudden bump and there was a stillness, except for

the movement made by the splashing water, and the three embryonic human beings jumped with hideous shouts on to the frozen land by the stake. The third one slipped as he landed, and the unholiness of his expletives was such that it could be understood in any language.

Now, now, quickly, his heart beating inside him like a drumbeat to prayer, Titus also jumped, and landed upright, nearly on top of the swearing villain who, judging from the cries of pain mingled with the swearing, must have broken his leg on landing. One thing Titus knew was that the creature would certainly receive no words of comfort from his two luckier companions.

He called out loud and clear, 'Dog!' The man lying on the ground stretched out his freezing hands and, as strong as an animal even in his own pain, he hit Titus with the side of his hand.

'Dog! – Dog! Kill him! Break his neck!'

The dog, which had been so gentle with the tiny child, was now ready to tear limb from limb the enemy of Titus.

The evil creature lying on the ground with all its venom hooked his arm round Titus's leg as he jumped to the icy surface. Titus fell as helplessly as a storm-tossed tree. He knew that he was done for. His strength was failing him, he had no reserves as the weakness laid him low, and the two companions followed, as night and day, their brutal companion in aiming blows at Titus. He was theirs to kill, but they reckoned without his canine companion, who had meant nothing but a stew and a warm coat to them.

'Dog!' cried Titus.

Growling, Dog jumped dextrously in the twilight, and a screech of pain followed; the villain's wrist had been bitten, his neck had been broken. In the end it becomes a matter for each being to survive and, as the darkness became more dense, so did the knowledge of defeat in the two remaining villains rend the air. Titus and his saviour drew away in stumbling steps, limbs jellified, panting and eager for life.

13

They Reach the Archipelagos and Forests

Titus and his dog ran away from the viciousness that nearly overcame them and lay hidden. An awareness of a more dulcet air grew. The ice was no longer present. A faint murmuration instilled itself; what were the voices they heard, what were the sounds? The shapes? Monkeys . . . parrots . . . birds of paradise . . . squirrels. Was it a dream? Was it paradise with hunger gnawing at their bellies? Was it freedom? Where were they? How had they reached this balm?

Titus felt the soft muzzle tickling his cheeks. Dawn, in all its ridiculous glory, began to show man to dog – and man to his surroundings. In their descent from the mountain and the icy cold they had reached a more comforting world. They were no longer frozen, and the great pale vermilion sun peered secretively (almost as though it would disappear if it disliked what it saw) over and into a world that Titus had forgotten existed. He saw the green of life, there was water, there was beauty in the strings of islands, which seemed to stretch to infinity. Each island was shaped differently; some like porpoises or dolphins as they surface, only to disappear again. Some islands were so elongated that you could not see where they ended; some squat and ugly; such mysterious dark shapes in the dawn, the sky sometimes aflame, sometimes so pale that the sea and itself were united.

To eat seemed imperative and as the light became more brilliant, Titus looked about him. He was reminded of his visit to Flay – poor banished Flay – so long ago. Flay had made a life for himself in his solitary existence. He had learned to hunt, to build fires, to feed himself, to clothe himself. 'Dog, if Flay could learn, so can I, so can you. There are many arguments against killing, but now is not the time for debate. We need to eat if we want to live. What do you see, Dog, where is our prey? Alive now, and unaware of our presence. With your paws I thee follow. With my eyes and with my hands I thee feed, with my brain I will discover the dreadful means by which we will live. Such cruelty, Dog, is in us when survival is the key. An orchestra plays in our empty stomachs – rumble, rumble, drums, rumble on. How long and how far can we listen to the rumbling? As long as it takes our initiative to find a way of assuaging that rumbling and the drumming in our stomachs becomes muted. There must be fish in this water and we must fish for them. Some happy fish, swimming about, is going to die for us. Perhaps some bird, with all its plumage – its glorious feathers plucked for us, and its naked skin pocked from where the feathers made it into a bird – will feed us, tough or tender as may be. How close to primitive man are we when we desire to live?'

Titus, with his eyes sharp as pine needles, saw the trees – he would find bait and make a hook – the green trees, some twisted and some with fronds hanging from them as though eager to catch the fish. 'Dog, help me to pull that frond which bends, then we must find one even more delicate.'

Titus pulled and pulled, but the frond clung to life as madly and with as much strength as the fish swimming unaware of its fate.

The dog had disappeared with the suddenness of a fog descending on an unsuspecting day, where the sun glowered.

A terrible sense of aloneness enveloped Titus and he suddenly foresaw, with an appalling intensity, the emptiness of a life led only to survive from day to day. Titus had felt that he had no need for patter, for parlance, for the rigmarole of society, but a life of only basic food, water, warmth without companionship would be meagre.

In the meantime the most urgent need was to survive. Even raw meat, raw fish, seemed palatable to Titus. But his thoughts raced back to his childhood. Dim, distant memories, of a boy, older than the rest, more knowledge-able in the lore of self-survival, who began to teach his companions the art of fire-making without which they might have frozen to the marrow. He almost forgot Dog's absence as these remembrances surfaced.

He searched around him for a blunt stick, until he came upon one that seemed right enough to rub back-wards and forwards on another piece of wood lying like a sacrifice upon the ground. He remembered his friend of long ago, issuing orders to his satellites, to rub and rub until their arms ached and the stick lying on the ground had a groove made in it. They didn't really know how it suddenly happened when a spark, a little miracle of red heat, appeared at the tip of the mutilating stick, and their commander quickly took it and laid it under the neatly stacked wood already waiting to be ignited. It was cold in the forest, but gradually, gradually, a glow from underneath the pile began to warm them, and Titus remembered the screeches of joy that cleaved the air, from the throats of his young, frightened compan-ions. Another memory that came to him was the command to keep a smouldering stick, so that the effort of lighting another fire would be eased, and to keep it smouldering, so that when the weather became damp, it would still be possible to light.

So Titus searched until he found, and built a small pyre – from branches, snapped briskly, because there was no rain – and he built, and he built, and he rubbed and rubbed, until once more, as years ago, the small red spark appeared and soon the pyre from sudden beginnings of rose colour began to crackle with sound. There was neither wind nor rain as the smoke mixed with the fire and spiralled upwards. Since leaving the hut of the lovers with his dog, he had not felt so warm, and now his anxiety, which had been quelled by his concentration in making the fire, became paramount. He missed his dog. If to no human being he could show the success of making fire, at least he should to Dog.

'I am quite alone now.'

As Titus said this to himself there was a cry of pain and the undergrowth being parted, and Dog appeared carrying an animal in his mouth and laid it at Titus's feet.

14

Lagoons – Fires

So fire had been learned – skinning had been learned – the barbaric acts of survival had been learned. No longer did the plucking or the skinning of the beautiful nauseate. So close is barbarity to civilisation.

Titus and his hound rested themselves, in the knowledge that they could now both survive where they were, until impetuosity, necessity, or the sheer desire to move bade them take to other shores, or other lands or peoples, for whom Titus was beginning increasingly to find a need. He had forgotten the physical desire for a woman, while he lay by the waning fire he felt he was no longer a man. When he thought of a woman, he could hardly envisage one. He took a stick and, oppressed by loneliness, drew upon the earth a woman.

No skill, no subtlety – breasts to suckle and breasts for suckling, round, pink-nippled, he made with tiny pink stones; a waist, and then that most urgent of all womanhood, plundered by man. Frustrated, he ceased drawing and lay face down on the coral-coloured earth, wept until all feelings ceased. His dog, who sensed every deprivation of his master, would lie at his feet after his morning's hunting and remain silent, until Titus was stirred by physical hunger of another kind.

'We have been gradually moving, Dog, and that water we see ahead of us has the tang of salt in it. Our diet will be saved. Salt is as much a part of my diet as a woman. It savours, it flavours, it adds desire to the beauty of this coral land. Even so, I want other company and when it comes I shall want it to go. I shall want to flee from it. I am no longer, or perhaps never was, a part of the human race.'

During the days Titus searched for a tree, blown down by the elements, that with rough hand-hewn tools he could fashion into a boat, which could negotiate the lagoons to which they had unwittingly drifted.

He made one and with long poles for oars he sat in it and glided with the grace of a swan on the water, and his one and only companion howled with despair, thinking that he was to be left alone.

'Oh, how cruel I am. Where has that desire come from that wishes to hurt?'

Titus drifted back and Dog, as the tree trunk edged

itself to the shore, put one paw tentatively, and then his other fearingly, then gently lowered his two back legs into the boat, until he attained his position as sentinel.

The sun, along with so many other things, made its gleaming way on to Titus's face and his hands, and poured solace over man and beast. They drifted in and out of waters, close to coral reefs, hunting, fishing, making fires. Titus sang, and Dog howled with the abandon that comes but seldom, with an awareness of the glories that life can hold but manifests with solemn rarity.

They drifted, and the beauty surrounding them became almost commonplace. Titus's hair began to burnish, and his face to tan – his body emanated a sensuousness to which there was no woman to respond. In the heat of the afternoon he pulled in, stripped off the remnants of what few clothes he had left and lay in the sun, and then with the dog he sought the shade, and they lay with arms and legs and paws outstretched, with their own respective dreams and the sounds that come from sleep – the heavy breathing, the calling from a distant subconscious and the balm of sleep – names from the past, sights, the illness of the past, and sometimes an echo that might be an intimation of the future.

Only hunger roused them.

The boat lilted up and down, with the ease of a craftsman. Titus awoke as the sun cooled, and he searched for his remnants of clothing. It took less time for his dog to position himself on the craft than for Titus to pull on his rags, and their drift in the dusk began again.

∘ ∘ ⊙ ∘ ∘

'I am cold.'

Ahead was the sinister vermilion. Fire. No longer did the sun warm them. They were cold, yet felt the heat. The flames performed the most skilled permutations of movement that could be imagined. The flames tore upwards to the sky, raging, tormented, tormenting, and the sound of heat coming through the air was terrifying; it was the crackling of ancient tribes, the scream of a hare torn to pieces, the violence inflicted by religion on its heretics. It was far away and it was beautiful. Its colour, unknown, unlearned by any artist. It was a distant sight and distant sound, yet where they were anchored Titus and his dog lay in silence, terrified.

Because the fire was far enough away Titus could afford to philosophise. Any closer he and his companion might well have been reduced to charcoal. 'Is all beauty hurtful?' he wondered, remembering the damage done to the walls of Gormenghast by the creeper in all its red and gold glory.

'Oh, Dog, let us go in another direction, away, away from it all. We might chance upon something we recognise.'

15

Among the Soldiers

A gale, over life-size, limbered up on the two pathetic exiles. Their boat was tossed, they were sick. Titus lay weakened from hunger, wandering, cold, despair, but there is always a hope, hidden subterraneously. Hope keeps man alive amidst all horrors. Even in the worst of men there is a little weakness, a flicker of hope, whether it be stirred by the golden hair of a child, or the grey hair of age, or some long forgotten memory. It was one such harsh man who descended on the river and drifted silent and mysterious as any ghost.

Hearing the sounds – a rhythmic moaning – he trod gingerly in the direction of the river, pushing the mist away from him as though it were a gauze curtain. His voice, used to command, was tossed by the wind into a parody of a voice, until it reached Titus's ears like the sound of frogs at night, insistent, harsh, removed from his experience.

Dog lifted his head painfully, alert to the new sound, so the croak drifted once more through the topsy-turvy mist, and Dog moved his right paw, and gently tapped Titus's cheek.

The voice of the man reached Dog again and in reply he let out an unearthly howl.

It generated knowledge in both, and curiosity in both: who or what would find the answer first? The man had the advantage, in that he had no care for any living soul but his own. Dog had the advantage in that he had the care of a living soul and, in his tactile way, exhausted as he was, that living soul was more important to him than anything else in his small circumscribed world.

The man was a soldier, a man used to issuing commands and to being obeyed. Behind the mist were a group of men, rough and used to hard living, to all the elements that nature can devise. They warmed themselves and threw their untidy shadows across each other by a fire on which was stretched the body of a suckling pig.

Laughs and whistles, a song, a harsh command from one man to another broke through to the man in the mist. He knew the men he commanded. The vilest of them was putty to him. 'Oh, let them sack and burn and prey – laugh, rape and be gay, but when the time comes and I say "stop" or when the time comes and I say "go" then they will. I have only to whistle to them and they will, like automata, rush to my bidding, but I want to discover the source of this sound, this nebulous lament. What I do with what I have found is of importance to no one but myself.'

Dog yelled. His voice eerie as a foghorn, reached the soldier, master of men. His howl broke through the darkness and the dim shape was silhouetted, black against grey with its jaws open.

The master of men clutched the silhouette in his mind's eye and, forcing his way with blade on felt under-growth, he ran with utmost clumsiness towards the howl.

He came to the sound – water lapping, a panting, both of fear and achievement – and the strong wind was enough to part the veil dividing them for the master of men to see a ghostly Dog. He leaned across the nettles and the eggs in nests to touch until the creature surren-dered to the hand of man.

Dog was the first to perceive that if not a friend at least not an enemy was at hand. His howl became more frenzied, as he sought the voice that shouted in an unknown tongue. The man yelled orders to the men behind him to come – one or two of them to help him reach forward to waylay the wandering bark before it was lost in darkness.

Crude men who had dined off their suckling pig wiped their hands across their lips, until the grease dripped down their unshaven chins leaving a trail, like the silver line made by a snail on its slow peregrinations from one purposeful destination of its own to another.

They had heard the voice of the man who commanded them and had no wish to concede to his commands, but his natural authority forced them to draw lots in their own way, which was to order the two youngest members of their group to forge into the darkness towards the water.

They carried burning torches but made no sound, except that of heavy boots threading and treading their way uneasily over lianas and twisted boles, night creatures scuttled in every direction unaccustomed to the smell of humans. Furtive and frightened, the two young men didn't dare make their presence known to the man who dominated everything and every person with whom he came in contact. Fear harassed them. Each could sense the pumping of the other's heart. It wasn't the quickening throb that a beautiful woman can induce; it was the same organ but a different song. Trembling with fear, the two untried youths walked towards their mentor.

The shrill and despairing yell of Dog sounded through the forest as far as the revelling soldiers, surfeited on suckling pig, who lay grossly, coarsely, lecherously around the dying fire and made its way into their scarcely alive subconscious. Then, having heard it, they relapsed into drunken inertia, and left to the chosen young all decisions as to how to find the yelps and cries for help.

At last they heard the voice of command and, because of their own lack of confidence, they ran, tripping, falling, swearing, once more towards authority.

'Quick – my men – shine your flares, we are reaching the unknown.' Dog's throat, hoarse with its demand, almost made its last appeal – smaller and more pitiful as though buried under the debris of an earthquake, a voice that had almost given up hope, tiny and defeated.

The flare picked up unknown silhouettes, and the sounds coming from the moving hulk were diminishing in as eerie a way as footsteps, lone footsteps, in the silence of the night disappear and make themselves heard to new ears, passing into new silence and out again.

'Quick – one of you hold both flares and the other one come to my aid.'

The command rang out and one of the young men hastened towards the voice, giving the flare to his companion.

'Here, here, hold fast to this hulk.' The sound of the water in the silence was mysterious and the man in command tripped over a liana, and as he fell he caught hold of one of the vines and almost fell into the river.

'Come here, you fool – you idiot,' and a string of obscenities followed, tracking its way into the dithering jelly of a youth who had no idea what to do.

'Hold my legs – tell that jackass to give us light.'

Suddenly the flares picked out a body lying spread-eagled, arms outstretched and holding with all its strength to the sides of the bank. In the gory light of the flare, the face appeared ashen, with the lips moving – a somnambulist upside down, lost and sleep-talking, and as the goldness moved over the body, leaving it in darkness, it tracked its way to the poor whimpering dog – tongue hanging out, but still poised to protect to his last whimper the living being he was guarding.

'Come on, you fools!' shouted the commander, and as he shouted and pulled at the boat, one of the young men in his nervousness dropped one of the flares into the water and the sound of the sizzling awakened the sleeper who called out in an unknown language, but Dog understood and made his way precariously towards his master to assuage his fear.

The commander wrenched Titus ashore. 'Go back, you fools, and bring a plank covered with your capes, and two more men and more flares. Take the only flare there is left now and leave us in darkness, but return using my instructions for warmth, and soup and shelter for whatever, or whoever we have here. And hurry, you fools!'

16

Still Among the Soldiers

The foolish young men wended their way quickly. Out of their commander's earshot, they tripped and swore. The slightly stronger of the two repeated the commands they had heard issued so recently, but his word didn't carry authority. They both knew that speed and the return with their undoubtedly inebriated seniors was crucial.

Poor young men, with so little experience, except perhaps of rather innocent debauchery, they stumbled and they sang, and they swore, and they gavotted towards the dying embers of a fire, around which they knew they would have to bring the immigrants or intruders to their camp.

In disarray, with no presiding genius to instruct them on how to assemble a stretcher from the rough materials at their command, they swayed and swirled towards long lengths of poles, which could form the handles on which to bear the body towards sanctuary.

A roughly made stretcher grew precariously and amateurishly, and with capes stretched across and lashed together with lianas it appeared to be strong enough to take a human body. The silliness and facetiousness of the young soldiers increased as they performed their task, and the one who had taken command with so little effect issued a giggling order to advance, which so infuriated the one to whom it had been addressed that he raised the cape stretcher and brought it down on the head of his non-commanding officer, who appeared to go through it, as a dog through a covered hoop in a circus. No applause accompanied the spectacle.

While this pathetic charade was being enacted, Titus still lay sprawled, neither knowing nor caring whether he lived or died, but Dog lay on the bank knowing and caring. The commander, frustrated by having no one to direct, save an unknown male of no known place of origin, paced the uneven ground with energy and petulance more suitable to a frustrated schoolmistress than a leader of men.

A light appeared to the south – only a tiny halo as glimpsed on the head of an Italian Baby Jesus, it couldn't throw any light on the surroundings, but it was sign enough for the hungry man of action awaiting the return of his men to the river bank.

As the halo hovered and made its way, lingeringly as

a lover's kiss, towards the darkness, the sounds that accompanied it also made themselves heard. There was not the same religious calm about the sounds as the sight. Indeed, there was a degree of instability in the sound. When two young men given authority for the first time come to use it, they must be forgiven for a certain amount of misuse. They had managed between them to seduce four more inebriated young huskies, who had been lolling in the firelight with nothing to do, to act as stretcher-bearers by the promise of illicit traffic in women, drugs and gold.

It was the sound of these six voices that the man among men heard and he cried out at the thought of action. But it was too soon, for the only sound the bearers could hear was the cracking dry undergrowth and an expletive of rage when an overhanging branch snapped back into an eye or an arm or a chest of a fellow soldier.

But as men digging a tunnel for years from opposing directions know that at some time they will meet, so with the same intensity of feeling did the seven men concerned in this rescue operation know that the light would glimmer in the darkness on the unknown wanderer and their own commanding officer.

As the time of fusion came there was no excitement, no sense of achievement, just ennui that there was only a vagrant and his dog as reward. Nevertheless, the stern voice of command acted upon the four stretcher-bearers and their two puerile leaders with the intensity of a rainstorm after a month of drought. Any inebriation they might have felt was quickly dispelled, and at the sound of 'Well, come on then, look to it, you curs' they ran to attention, as though being chased by an infuriated cockerel.

The two young officers held the flares which lit up Titus's body, and the stretcher-bearers laid the roughly made haven on the ground by the exhausted man. Dog whined but seemed to sense that there was no harm intended at that moment. Orders were issued to deal gently but expediently with the body of the exhausted man and he was lifted with rigid care on to the roughly made bed by the four young recruits who had no knowl-edge of the gentle arts and displayed very little consid-eration for the wellbeing of the stricken and foreign wanderer.

By dint of youth and strength they lifted him on to the stretcher, and a sigh that would have shattered more sensitive mortals vibrated against the undergrowth. The man among men raised his voice for the stretcher party to advance, and Dog yelped in thanksgiving for his master's deliverance.

The flares were raised overhead and an uncanny light

led the procession onwards and away and back. The return journey was slow and stumbling, interspersed by crude expletives, while Dog faithfully brought up the rear.

17

Back at Camp

Dawn was breaking as the party entered the clearing. The flares had been extinguished, as nature was well enough equipped to throw a dramatic light on the characters in the play. The players acted the parts assigned to them despite the almost unbearable fatigue felt. First their duty was to lay the foreigner in a bivouac and cover him with rugs, and let him sleep away the past and the present, until his stirring would lead him into a future. Dog lay exhausted at his feet.

The officer commanding had plans for this unknown captive. Titus knew nothing of these plans, but he was, as he hovered between dream and reality, tiring of forever being rescued, forever owing his being to others. He did not count Dog, for he was on the same side. He heard voices that spoke a language he could not fathom, but he was becoming used to belonging nowhere. 'This is self-imposed,' he thought hazily. 'It always has been. I want no one. I need no one, and I shall neither give nor take, except when the giving and the taking are for mutual self-satisfaction. Why should I not leave Dog here, as I have wanted to leave him before in other places. Somewhere within me there must be a chink of what others might call humanity, or love or – or – or,' and he sank again, dreaming of a world where he was beholden to no one, and where his physical strength was no longer warped by hunger and cold.

Titus awoke one morning with the eyes of a stranger upon him. Cold and hard eyes, small like a rhinoceros in a face of crinkled grey leather, that were so vicious and intelligent that the hardness Titus had thought he possessed evaporated as though it had never existed, and he put out his hand for comfort to touch Dog.

Words as harsh as the eyes were spat at him, then a gesture he interpreted as 'Get up', for they were followed by the unceremonious peeling of the bed coverings. The chill of contempt hit him as hard as the chill of the day, as his body lay semi-nude and defenceless in front of the iced-leather face. He made to cover himself, as had the many girls in the past covered their breasts in front of him. Fleetingly Titus understood that what he had always thought of as a coy and provocative gesture in them was actually a wish to belong to themselves, until they succumbed to a sensation of which they were no longer mistress.

He felt unclean and depraved and, as his temper rose, so did he attempt to rise and pull back the coverings, which the creature had wrested from the bed. Dog crouched, awaiting a word, but infected also by the tension that warped the air. A thin laugh, like the scraping of chalk on a blackboard, reached Titus and fed his irrational hatred towards the unpleasant character who looked down upon him.

Titus's barely concealed arrogance broke through and he rose, defying his nakedness and his weakness, and leaned towards the malevolent eyes, hitting the leather face with a powerless fist, exhausting the small reserve of energy that he had been hoarding. He fell back, drained by the unexpected effort.

Titus knew what he had done was foolish, without stratagem and something for which he would certainly pay – but in what way?

Night came and the sounds of night with it. The human sounds of male voices, some raucous, some raised above the others in a rich baritone or a bass so deep that it all but merged with the darkness. Firelight flickered and the smell of roasting meat filled Titus with a hunger that betokened his early return to health.

He had been fed and cared for, and whereas before he had wished to recompense his saviours for their charity, he now wished to escape from what he feared might lead to an intrusion on his liberty. For he knew that he was in a military camp and he had a suspicion that he was to be used in some plot as yet to be revealed.

He did not wish it to be known that his strength was returning, yet his hunger became unbearable as it rampaged through his body, and the one and only thought in his mind was how it could be assuaged. It was too dangerous to show himself, but more than he could bear to stay confined and inert.

His problem was resolved more quickly than he might have hoped. 'Old Rhino Eyes', as Titus called him to himself, appeared with no ceremony and raised his voice to two figures outside who were waiting for a command, which was given to them by the peremptory clapping of two hands, as dry and hard as inflammable tinder.

The whiffs of roast meat glided in and through and over Titus, so that his mouth almost filled with its imaginary juices, and it took a self-control he hardly knew he possessed not to dribble the overflow down his beard, which had grown during his delirium.

A table was brought and laid by two men dressed in white, and a chair was placed on either side of the table. A gown was given to Titus of an ordinary dark brown wool and Old Rhino Eyes with mock bows and courtesy indicated that Titus should robe himself and be seated. With difficulty he pulled on the robe and with as little loss of dignity as possible he put his unused limbs to work. He felt the mean little eyes on his every movement, and the dilemma of wanting to appear both weaker than he felt and yet strong enough to eat was rather more than his intellectual resources could cope with. However he resolved it, the eyes were X-raying him whether he liked it or not, so that he decided to empty his mind, in order that it should not give him away in any degree.

Titus sat with relief on the chair and recoiled at the hospitality he was about to receive from one whom he had so recently but ineffectually struck.

One of the men dressed in white appeared, carrying a plate and a covered dish, which he placed on the table in front of Titus, who noticed that despite the two chairs there was only one place laid for eating. He immediately felt at a disadvantage – eating alone, under scrutiny, nullified the pangs of hunger that had recently surged through him. The distant past of his childhood, where ornate, almost architectural meals had been served and left to crumble untasted, flitted across his mind and then the sordid and mean meals that he had scrounged in his journeyings over the past ten years superimposed themselves, and he felt that he no longer wished to eat and give away that primitive part of his being to Rhino Eyes. He remembered, with disgust, a hyena he had seen

93

fighting one of its own kind over the membrane of a newly born zebra, too frail to get away, which they had torn into, in all its bright pink rubberiness, and the unholy sound of their glutinous chewing.

'Eat.' His host appeared to gesture, as the lid of the dish was lifted by one of the white-robed men. Dog lay on the ground by Titus and, following his master's restraint, lifted only his eyes to watch. Titus indicated that his canine companion should also be fed and with a clap of his hands the rhino-eyed autocrat ordered that this should be done. A plate was put in front of Dog, but he made no movement until Titus, with a supercilious gesture belying his hunger, lifted a fork and toyed with what he imagined to be a most tender suckling pig; then Dog, with his muzzle, almost like an echo, played with the food on his plate, which was of the same quality as his master's.

This pantomime began to annoy the man, who sat opposite Titus, awaiting the weakness of his captive guest. Impatiently he urged him to eat. He plainly wished to see Titus in a subservient position, and when Titus merely played with the food in front of him, the creature indicated that there would be no more hospitality, the plates were removed and he left the table imperiously, followed by the two men in white.

Titus, almost weaker than before he came to table,

rose and practically fell, his head dizzy with hunger and drowsiness, yet he felt that he had scored a victory, but how it could be used he was uncertain. Still, as he limped his way back to his bed, he knew he must plan to escape the servitude he felt was being prepared for him.

18

Plans of Escape

Later that night the fitful sleep, compounded of gnawing hunger and a dizziness both spiritual and temporal that had enveloped Titus and to a lesser degree Dog, was gently interrupted by the faintest sound. It was a cold night, a supernatural ice immobilised Titus. At the slight movement of the flap of the tent the ice melted within him, and his stomach muscles tautened and he moved one leg and then the other. A hand feeling for the opening of the tent, hardly to be seen in the darkness, groped tentatively and silently. Titus felt the soft paw of comfort on his arm, it was a communication that lessened his fear. No time for theory, no time for introspection; action was the only antidote to thought. Now was the time for action, if only the body's response was capable of smothering the traitor in his brain.

The flap of the tent opened more widely, and silently a form made itself felt, slithering like a grass snake along the ground until Titus was aware of the body beside his trestle bed. He knew that he had no friends in this camp and that there was no means of verbal communication. Who could it be? No enemy would come with such silence. Could it be one of the two white-clothed servitors who had placed food in front of him? They had seemed without character or personality – only ciphers to do what they were told by the imperious Rhino Eyes. Perhaps it was a look of barely perceptible compassion, rather than indifference, which one of them had cast at him as he had taken away the plate of food?

A hand grasped his hand as though for reassurance. It touched his face and traced the nose and mouth and chin as a blind man learns a face. Then Titus felt his hand being lifted and his fingers being led over the contours of the head and features belonging to the exploring hand, and as he touched the mouth, he felt the lips smile, not in hatred but in friendship, and within a moment the hand had gone, and all that belonged to it had gone, and Titus was left not knowing if he had dreamed the sensation or sensed a dream. He must have slept again, and awakened when the light began to filter through the tent.

As he lay waking, his foot moved and a faint sound of an object falling to the ground alerted him, and he turned his head to follow the sound. Wrapped in a dock leaf was what appeared to be a knife.

∘ ∘ ∘ ∘ ∘

For the next week, as Titus gathered strength, there were no visitations from anyone, except for two plates of rudimentary food to be placed outside the tent three times a day, then removed with as little ceremony.

Titus's plans to leave were progressing as his health improved but he had need of an ally to help him translate his thoughts into deeds. Dog might be a hindrance to him, he thought. He needed someone who knew the surrounding terrain and despite the fact that no force had been used on him, he was aware that he was a prisoner in all but name. Where was that man who had ventured so stealthily into his tent several nights earlier? Titus could not know that he was also a captive, and that when the next chance arose the man would come, also with hopes of escape. Day and night there was activity, which through lack of knowledge of the language Titus could only guess at. But that it was of a martial and aggressive nature there could be no doubt. The harsh voice of command must sound the same in any language, and the regimentation of men to whatever creed or philosophy, as demeaning to the individual spirit. There was no sound of firearms, but the sense of an oppressive mastermind at work lay heavily on him.

During the days when his strength had returned, Titus walked outside his tent. It seemed to be removed from the main area of the bivouacs, as though to mark it out and perhaps prevent any attempt at escape. There was only one larger tent close to his, and on his excursions he was bidden what he took to be a 'good morning' by Rhino Eyes, who stood at the opening flap of this tent and bowed in a sardonic gesture of respect. He realised that he was to be used as a decoy, but for what he did not know. By whom he was fairly sure. Titus knew that to circumvent this villain would take more knowledge, more cunning and more strength than he possessed.

The days were interminable and the nights scarcely less so. Each night at dusk, when the fires lit up the tent, the sense of isolation became intolerable. The sounds of men talking together, laughing and singing, interspersed with altercations between those who had imbibed too much liquor had a bonhomie that Titus both despised yet sought. Each night he thought that he would join the conviviality. Each night he argued against it, talking to his only companion, Dog.

One night there was an unnatural silence, with no firelight to lighten the gloom. His plate of food was left as usual outside his tent, but he had become morose and even the thought of food became obnoxious. On lifting the flap of the tent to remove the plate he saw beside it a flagon of red liquid. The idea of drink, which would perhaps dilute his weariness of soul, his sense of boredom, lifted his sense of fruitlessness. His sleeplessness might be assuaged by a flagon of wine.

'Dog, I shall put myself to sleep, despite the fact that I shall have to wake again, but I long for annihilation if only for a night.'

He took his plate and put it aside, and as he lay on his bed and held the flagon to his lips to fulfil this wish, he was aware of a movement, a sound, a feeling that he was no longer alone. By the pricking of Dog's ears he knew this to be so.

19

Escape

As Titus lifted the wine to swallow at a gulp as much of it as possible, the flagon was knocked out of his hand with a complete lack of ceremony and it was not until he found himself lying flat on his back, wine splashed about him with the profligacy of blood, that he connected the sensation of another being, close to him, with the unexpected overthrow of his wine, his road to Lethe.

The face that looked at him from the ground by his bed was the one he had been hoping would reappear and, as their eyes met, a terrible yearning for his distant past, the true love that he had abandoned, almost suffocated Titus, until he remembered that he was living here and now, and that there was a great problem to be overcome.

The eyes were close together, that much he could vaguely distinguish. Their reflection of earlier eyes set close together discomforted him, until a humorous intelligence came into them, and he perceived gestures in the gloom. A pantomime was being enacted. Hands criss-crossed at speed in front of his face, then a falling back into a deep sleep, after the mimed quaffing of the contents of the flagon, and the figure lay prone on the ground as if dead.

Titus understood from this charade that the wine had indeed been drugged and he understood at the same time the reason why. The silence that reigned around him was the silence of an empty camp. Surely now was the time to take his leave of the place, but he did not believe that Rhino Eyes would have left the way so clear for him to escape, even if he had taken the drink that was to have immobilised him.

The figure in the tent stood up, and Titus recognised one of the white-robed men who had put food in front of him and whose eyes had registered the minimum of compassion. It was also he who had paid the silent visitation to his tent. But why? Was he also a captive? Useless to ask, as there was no common tongue, only the language of the hands, the eyes, the body.

Titus stood up and, for the first time since he had been brought to the tent, felt the potential strength of his twenty-six years. His muscles were slack from lack of use, but he felt an exhilaration that had been sadly absent over the last months, an urge for action, to be master of his own fate.

With a gesture that signified haste, speed-flight, the man beckoned to Titus and Dog to follow him. Titus feared there was danger and that he might be following him into a wily trap. But there was something in the man's face which belied suspicion. He pushed the sleeve of his right arm up to his elbow, and deeply branded on the inside Titus saw a series of numbers and two letters. Was this a symbol of servitude? It was no good to stand asking questions that could not be answered, and Titus decided to follow. He had no possessions to hamper his departure, no love to leave, nothing familiar that would torment his going. He picked up the knife the man had left and stepped out into the dawning light, followed by Dog.

There was an uncanny silence, such as is felt in oppressive heat, when the sky darkens and a storm is awaited. No sounds of birds, or humans, no wind, no rain, no thing, nothing.

Titus saw what seemed to be a clearing in the darkness of a yew wood, where tents were pitched. This was where the camp was and where the voices, the laughter, the music and the expletives had come from, which he had heard when he had been lying in his tent. He had not imagined a yew wood. The silence added to its malignant darkness. The boles of the trees were deep red, gnarled and ancient, and the foliage black with age. This wood, these trees had seen the fortunes and the misfortunes of men over a thousand years, fugitives, violent death, fear, but very little love.

In the clearing, apart from the tents, was a house, incongruously neat, wooden and shuttered.

As the man gestured him to follow, Titus caught sight of a movement in the wood, and as he looked to see what else moved on this uncanny day, he saw a rat larger than any he had ever seen run into the darkness, followed by what must have been a family of rats on the move. Their tails were longer, he thought, than the one he could never forget, long ago, in another dark and sinister world.

These memories flashed by and were gone; it was not a time for brooding. With speed-man, Titus and Dog made for the clearing, and the house, passing the hut of Rhino Eyes. It could not have been inhabited, as Titus had thought. As they neared it, he saw that the shutters were hanging from their hinges, the windows were broken and there was a smell of dankness overall. Around the house was a veranda, with three steps leading up to it. A door was open and they went in. Broken furniture lay around, a table upside down, with the look of a dead horse lying on its back when rigor mortis has set in, only the stomach flat and empty. But another table had the remains of a meal on it, seemingly recent, for there was no mildew or smell of decay. A few rugs were scattered on the dust-laden floorboards, and in a cupboard with its doors ajar there hung what appeared to be military coats.

At the sight of the food Titus felt a sickness of hunger for he had almost forgotten what it was like not to feel hunger. There was bread, there was some kind of partly cooked meat and a jug.

With a courtesy that might seem surprising in a man who physically now resembled an emaciated brigand (during the weeks or months of his confinement his hair had grown to shoulder length and his beard strag-gled on to his chest) Titus offered the man, who was either his jailer or his deliverer, the plate of food.

Titus motioned to Dog to come forward. He placed on a plate some of the meat and put it on the floor, together with water from the jug. Then he helped himself to what remained, but found that his capacity for food was dulled, and what should have been a joyous consum-mation brought very little comfort to him. Dog ate his with a restraint that belied his canine ancestry, and finished when he saw that his master was no longer eating.

Titus knew that he was the most dominant of the

three, that it was for him to assume command, but he felt hampered by the lack of a communal language. Then he decided that he would speak in his own, and that by the very intonation of words he would make himself understood, if at the same time his words were accompanied by gesture. He remembered an old mischievous woman that he had met on one of his peregrinations, who had told him how she had mistaught a foreigner her own native language. To say 'good morning' she had taught her pupil to say 'broom-handle' – when she pointed to eyes, nose, mouth, feet, etc., she substituted the words salt, pepper, mustard, cabbage, and yet that teacher and that learner communicated with each other in a language they mutually understood, but no one else could.

But it was by intonation alone that Titus decided to speak.

'Come quick, we must go, while the camp is empty. Shall we see what clothes there are in the cupboard? Come on Dog and Man – quick.'

Still speaking, he went to the cupboard where soldiers' coats were hanging and the man, understanding, followed Titus, who gestured that he try on whatever he wanted, to ensure some kind of disguise. He felt that time was too precious to waste, but that it was vital to make some change in their appearance, despite the fact that there was no possibility of disguising Dog. He also knew that his hair and beard must be shorn, and that he must trust to the dexterity of his companion's use of a large sharp knife. He gestured to his hair and beard, with a cutting motion, and said in his own language, 'But that must wait. Come, let's put on our coats and hats.' So Titus pushed as much of his matted hair as possible into his woollen cap.

It was getting lighter – in fact, almost full daylight – as they left the empty house and silently went down the three steps from the veranda on to the mossy grass, before again plunging into the black gloom of the yew wood.

The man, whom Titus now thought of both as a friend and fellow captive, obviously had some knowledge of the woods. Left to himself, Titus would not have known which of the many paths to take. Although they were not paths as such, they were tracks, each one leading to a different future, all of them unknown. As he followed, with Dog close behind, he noticed the man rubbing each tree on the outside of the route they were taking. He gestured to know what was being done, and at the next tree the man pointed to an almost infinitesimally small white chalk arrow, to show them the way out of the forbidding wood, but whose obliteration would diminish the likelihood of anyone following.

The only sounds were the rustling of leaves above and the alarm calls of birds whose territory was being invaded, and the quick rush of a rat, as it ran from one hole to another.

Titus felt that the gloom of the yew wood would never lift – that there was no other world outside it. He could not envisage a time or place that did not surround him in darkness or where he could exchange conversation with people who understood not only what he was saying, but why and how.

They seemed to have walked for hours, but it was almost as though they had stayed in the same place, so little did the ambience change. Each tree, taken alone, was unique and thick with character, but one after another assumed the anonymous sameness of faces in a crowd, and he longed for a yew tree that betrayed its brothers by bright green foliage and silver bark.

As these thoughts passed inconsequentially through his mind, Titus was slowly growing aware of his head becoming lighter. But it was not his head, it was a glimpse of sky, penetrating the roof of yew, and as he looked ahead, he could see a doorway of emerald grass, and a chance to enter another world. Seeing such an invitation to throw off the gloom and the nothingness of his last months of grey inactivity, he felt his legs moving faster and faster towards the door of light, until he was running so fast that he almost tripped on the uneven criss-crossed path of ancient roots. Dog followed close, scenting his master's exuberance.

Titus stopped running for a moment, to see where their guide-man was and found that he was standing still, almost a fly in amber, dried white in the darkness, trapped. The man stood motionless, as Titus returned to him. He lifted the sleeve of his robe, and once more showed the numbers cut into his arm. He drew an imaginary knife across his throat, he spread his arms in what might have been hope or hopelessness and he turned back and ran as fleetingly as a leveret, back into the darkness from which the three of them had just emerged.

It was a moment of truth. Should Titus follow? What conscience he had told him it was what he should do; what reason he had told him of the pointlessness of such an action. Reason prevailed and, with Dog and an absence of guilt, he ran until he was out of the wood and sitting panting on the sunlit verge, where he fell into a deep sleep of nothingness. He only awoke on hearing in the distance what sounded like the baying of hounds, a pistol shot and a cry of pain.

20

An Unexpected Meeting

Titus and Dog found themselves on a narrow road in open countryside: downland, with clumps of bushes and neat fields; a huge expanse of sky, not blue, but grey-white, and convoluted clouds that changed their shapes at each blink.

Hunger, never at bay for long, began again to remind Titus that he was at the mercy of his own being. His ingenuity was once more called upon.

'Come on, Dog, let's see what we can find along the hedgerows – not that you will care for what nature provides there. Why don't you burrow and chase, and kill and eat? I have a knife and you have your whole elemental being.'

As they walked down the narrow road, towards what seemed to be a meeting of four roads, the man and his dog for all their hunger were breathing the air of freedom.

At the crossroads Titus stood and looked in all directions. He saw space and time, but he did not see which way he should take. In the middle of the cross was a heart-shaped island of grassy stubble, and for some reason of symmetry he sat in the middle of it, to empty his mind and to make a decision, with no recourse to logic, on which way he should go.

They must have sat on the heart-shaped mound for twenty minutes when Dog pricked up his ears before Titus could find the reason why. In the distance there was if not a sound of human life, at least a sound that was controlled by human life; a slow advent on to the scene of an alien-to-nature sound; an internal combustion engine that seemed to be contending with age, so much did it hesitate, blow and bang, stop and start again, long before it could be seen.

Surprise was no longer part of Titus's life. He had lived on the edge of it for so long. Curiosity he still possessed in abundance. Nothing was ever as it might be envisaged. Things were invariably more strange than the wildest imaginings.

'Do I always let things happen to me, then, Dog? Am I an onlooker or am I a catalyst? Am I a man whose childhood is incomprehensible to all but those who turn their back on this world because they cannot bear what it offers? Who am I, and what, or who is about to enter our lives? Can it be someone that will pass us by? Can it be someone who will change the course of our lives?

Shall I be master of my own fate, or should I leave it to fortune?'

This was not to be so easy: the spluttering car was upon him and almost annihilated him as it came to a stop in the middle of the heart-shaped island. He had just enough time to jump out of its way and as he landed face down on the road, he heard a sound of wheezing, together with a jumble of dry coughing and laughter. His first instinct was of anger, and his natural quick temper hastened his speed to turn, sit and stand up to whoever was the cause of his undignified collapse.

He had no idea what he might expect, but it was certainly not what he now saw. It was a woman of around thirty or thirty-five, small and thin, with short, dark hair so jagged it was seemingly cut with a razor. She had a little bony face, with smudged hazel eyes, a narrow, aquiline nose, and a small mouth with a half-smoked cigarette, which clung to her bottom lip like a limpet. 'I'm so sorry,' she said, hacking and chuckling. 'I think I dropped off to sleep – I've been driving all night, and only woke when the car stopped on the heart. A heartbeat, a car beat, be dat what it may, be-ware, be-troot, be good, be gone, bee-hive, b-awful . . . At least you're not hurt.'

'And I can see that you are not hurt either,' said Titus. He felt unable to compete with the verbal play of the strange woman. But the very thought of a woman, after so long a time of thinking of nothing but survival, made him look at her less as a person than as a symbol, of something which he had so often sought, so often treated roughly, but felt an unholy need of.

He began 'I'm not a wit . . .'

'Not a wit too soon . . .' and then followed another paroxysm of coughing and laughter, with cigarette smoke exhaling a delicate pale-grey blind between them.

'Oh, to hell with you – I'm in no mood for wordplay – hardly in any mood at all – who in hell are you? I'm Titus Groan – that's simple enough. I've had my fill of clever women. All I want, now that you've appeared from out of the blue, is to know where you are going, not where you have come from. I'm not interested. Can you help me, have you any food, have you a home, a house, a room, a bed, a floor? Just answer me quite simply, and if it's at all possible without the frills of smokes and coughs and laughter . . .'

It was so long since Titus had given outward expression to any thought that he was insensitive to the brusqueness and the roughness of his voice, and what it said, and when he at last looked at the small woman to whom he was speaking, he was surprised to see her lower lip, to which the cigarette still clung, trembling, and all the vividness of her personality extinguished.

'Now it is for me to say sorry. My harshness was not deliberate and I have no excuse. I am sorry. To blow out a candle that is shedding light in a dark room is thoughtless, unkind and stupid, and what's more makes life a good deal less interesting. Now I've talked too much. You say something.'

'Oh, that is the one thing that would really silence me, cough and all.'

'Well, at least I have told you my name. Cannot you tell me yours?'

'It's Ruth Saxon – quite straightforward, really – and if you get to know me better, you'll probably think it strange that there should be anything straightforward about me. Not that I'm crooked, but that I never seem to think or do things as other people do, or at least so my family tell me.'

'Then we should get on rather well,' said Titus in a conciliatory tone. 'Perhaps the same could be said about me.'

As they talked, probing circuitously each other's personalities, Titus had time to look at and into the car, which had so suddenly broken his solitude. It had a character to fit its owner. It was full of personality. Canvases lay in the back, piled one upon the other, stones and shells of all sizes were scattered on the seat behind the driver's, and sitting regally disdainful of outside events was a clowder of cats of varying colours, peering from behind a large bunch of wayside flowers.

'Yes, I'm a painter, and I love cats and I carry my heart on my sleeve. I love painting more than anything in the world. I love everything to do with it. The smell of turps, the materials I use, the brushes, the canvas, the silence, the solitude. When I'm painting I'm consciously serene. Perhaps it's the only time when I'm not asking myself insoluble questions. The sole truth when I'm painting is the truth of paint. It doesn't matter how old I become, it'll always be there, and some of the world's greatest painters reached their old age passionately living, their hearts, their eyes, their souls, their hands plying their trade. One old painter had an inscription on his grave: "Here lies an old man mad about painting." There, that tells you about me. What about you, Titus?'

'Perhaps I don't feel passionate about anything. You are one of the lucky ones. If I learn to know you better I will tell you about my life, but you may not believe me. Let my life emerge slowly and you can judge me as it unfolds. Perhaps I am doomed to be an onlooker. But at any rate, before we probe too deeply, just tell me where you were going and perhaps our ways might take the same route, at least for a short time. I'm not one to stay too long in any place.'

'Well, I've been down to the beach to pick up the

stones you can see in the car, and I'm on my way back to my studio. Would you like to come with me and stay a while? I love my studio, but I'm afraid there's not a great deal of comfort. I haven't much money and I can't cook, and I like being alone; and what's more, you can bring your companion with you, who has been so patient while we've been exploring each other's whims.'

'What about the cats, though?'

'Well, as you can see, very little can disturb their complete and utter self-absorption. What is his name?'

'Dog.'

'Dog?'

'Yes, Dog.'

'Why?'

'Well, he's not a cat.'

'He's not a giraffe either.'

'If I don't give him a name, I feel I'm not responsible for him.'

'I don't like that.'

'Nor do I.'

'Don't you, Titus?'

'No.'

'I have a name, you know.'

'Yes, I know.'

'Can't you say it?'

'I can say it.'

'But won't you?'

'I will some time.'

'You don't have to be responsible for me if you use it, you know, Titus. It makes me feel as though I'm not here, and I'm all here, and there, and by and large, and to and fro, and my name is Ruth. Say it, please.'

'Ruth.'

'Now we can get on our way, Titus. Let's clear a space in the car, so that poor Dog can get in on the seat, and you can sit in front. But can you wait a moment? We've got a longish drive ahead and perhaps we had all better go behind the bushes. You take Dog and I'll be back in a minute.'

When they all met again, Titus had waited to clear the car, for he didn't want to disturb the cats without their mistress being there.

It need not have worried him for apart from a lazy stretching and re-disposition of their bodies into more comfortable positions, their self-possession was not disturbed. Titus told Dog to get in, and even when his large frame clambered on to the back seat the cats did not display more than cursory interest. He was not an enemy. Dog had learned much patience and much tolerance since he had been with Titus.

∘ ∘ O ∘ ∘

S omehow, on even such a short knowledge of Ruth, Titus could not imagine her behind the wheel of a car. The two seemed incompatible. This car was unlike Muzzlehatch's, although he had also been incongruous, and so much bigger than life – his ape, his animals, the very essence of his being. This remembrance trembled on the edge of Titus's consciousness before he returned to the present, and he became curious as to how Ruth and the car would come to terms with each other.

It was rather as he had imagined, as the door closed behind her and almost with a leap the car sprang into action, grunting and wheezing and jerking as though in the throes of an epileptic fit.

'I don't really like cars; in fact, I hate them. Treat 'em rough, as my father used to say about anything and everything that didn't belong to him. I don't understand them but I don't want to either. So long as we get from one place to another in one piece, that's all they're for.'

Titus was well able to agree, for he had never owned a car or wanted one. His way of life had no need of possessions – he had renounced the shackles that posed a threat to his freedom, but now was not the time for him to turn over introspectively the whole of his past life; for the time being he gave himself up to the present, and the fact that he was with a woman, a woman quite unlike any he had met before. Not a feminine woman, too thin and wiry and unconscious of her sex to be a womanly woman. Not flirtatious, not filled with guile, she was companionable and humorous, but Titus felt she was vulnerable and quickly hurt.

They drove along the narrow country road with intermittent bursts of speed and sluggishness, but whether that was at the whim of the driver or the questionable ability of the engine Titus could not tell. They didn't talk but there was no sense of embarrassment in the silence. Ruth seemed abstracted and thoughtful, and not thinking of what impression she might be making on the man who sat next to her.

The landscape was changing from the rural richness of downland and fields and hedgerows to a more urban morose greyness. They had turned into a wider road and there was now a continuous cavalcade of cars in each direction, and no mercy shown to the moody car, which did not belong to the stream of rapid sleek machines that continually passed them.

'It's about another half-hour's drive,' said Ruth. 'I hope you're not too hungry. We can't stop even if we wanted to, even if there were any food, even, if, even, only, even, even, un-even, even-tide, even-song, songbird and so on, and on, and on, until we get there, and how I want to be there. My home. Close the door and shut out the world, but take parts that I like with me. Oh, come on, car, take us home – quick, quick.'

Little grey houses now hemmed in the cars. Unlovely and all alike, except for an occasional burst of personality, when the window frames and door had been painted mauve or yellow, or red or green.

'It's not far now,' said Ruth. 'Soon we turn off, and although the studio has no architectural beauty, as soon as the door is closed we enter a new world, or rather one where I feel safe. Whatever you think of "Home", that's what I think, love and the things that I love, you'll soon see. What do you think "Home" means, Titus?'

'Well, that is too big for me to answer in a short time. If you allow me to stay for a little while, I will tell you about my childhood and my name.'

'Why should I query your name? You didn't query mine.'

Ruth turned the car from the mean and ugly road into a much wider road, which seemed to be a cul-de-sac. It was not a particularly beautiful road, except that at the end of it there stood, almost as sentinels, a group of chestnut trees. The large building by which the car stopped, as suddenly and jerkily as it had taken off, was gaunt, grey and windowless. About eight steps led up to a door, which appeared to be permanently ajar and as Ruth opened the car door the cats flew out, up the steps, through the door and into the darkness beyond.

Dog, being a guest like his master, waited to be told what to do, and as Titus followed Ruth out of the car, so too did he.

'We'll go in first, and then I wonder if you could help me, Titus, bring in the treasure trove I've got in the car.'

'I'll take some now.'

'No, I'd rather show you my home first, then we can bring it in.'

As they ascended the steps and went through the doors there was very little light, but Titus sensed a long corridor, with doors at equal intervals along it, for from under one or two of them appeared a light, and some sounds of music or laughter or argument seeped out, and from behind one door a smell of cooking, which reminded Titus that his last meal and that of Dog had been in an empty house in a dark, unfriendly yew wood, and he had a pang of remorse as he thought of his guide and his unknown fate.

At the end of the long passage was another door facing them and Ruth said, 'Well, here we are.'

'Where are the cats?' asked Titus.

'They have their own special door,' said Ruth, as she fumbled in what must have been a letterbox and drew forth a long length of string, with a key attached to the end of it, with which she opened the door to her domain.

She switched on a light, and as the room was drained of its darkness Titus's heart thumped at what he saw.

His memory flew back to a series of attic rooms, where his sister had collected all that she loved best in life, and which she had guarded fiercely from intrusion.

The room he looked at now was a ferment of so many things that he could take in no detail, only the overpowering 'feel' of the place. One wall was a huge window, divided into large rectangular panes of glass, and the other three walls were covered with paintings, framed and unframed drawings, books, photographs cut from papers of animals, birds, mountains, people's faces, clowns, masks and spears. A piece of seaweed hung from some kind of hook on the wall, and there were stuffed birds on shelves and tables. Tables, with paints and brushes, stood near two enormous easels and on the floor were stones and carvings of wood and stone. Leaves and half-dead flowers in poor arrangements stood incongruously on a table that must have served for eating on, for plates and teacups stood on sheets of paper with writing and drawings on them, and sitting on a mound of paper was one of the cats who had been a passenger with Titus in the car. Another had climbed and found a niche on a windowsill and sat looking out, with teeth chattering at the sight and sound of small birds, flying from branch to branch outside, but not within range of the sudden pounce.

The ceiling was cathedral high and in one corner of the studio stood a large black stove, with a thick black pipe that disappeared far above into the ceiling. It was unlit, but it had so much character that it was a personality in its own right, standing ominous and full of potential. In another corner, almost incidentally, was a bed, covered with a patchwork quilt, on which lay another ubiquitous cat.

'Oh, dear,' cried Ruth, cigarette dancing up and down as her lip quivered. 'You are hungry – I am hungry – Dog is hungry – cats are hungry, but I'm so tired too. Which comes first?'

'Well, at the risk of seeming vulgar, I am hungry, first and foremost, and then tired. What is there to eat? Can I help – have you any food, is there a stove – is there anywhere to cook anything?' asked Titus.

'You haven't seen quite all yet,' answered Ruth. 'I will show you what there is, then we can make what we can of it. Come on outside and you will see the extent of my domain.'

Titus followed her as she opened the door of the studio and led him into the corridor, and on the opposite side to the door went up three or four dark stairs to another door, which opened on to a smallish room with a huge window, with no outlook, but a steep brick wall. There was what appeared to be a bath, covered by a large wooden board, and a black cooking stove. Ruth made for a green-painted cupboard, which she opened almost hesitatingly. Some apples, onions, bread, butter, a dark cake, eggs – not exactly haute cuisine – but enough to satisfy the hunger of two adults and one large dog. The cats, being cats, made sure that their needs had already been seen to.

Without finesse, both Ruth and Titus made use of what there was to hand, and fed themselves and Dog. When all three needs were satisfied, they went back to the studio and, without question, without coyness or sensuality, they threw off their clothes and dropped exhausted on to the low and rather lumpy bed.

21

An Affectionate Welcome

When Titus awoke, he was aware of a slight weight on his chest and, opening his eyes, he met the steady gaze of two yellow ones and a sound of what he thought had been a distant beat of drums. His feet were also constricted, and as he moved to free them a cat sailed gently into the air and landed in a hollow of the bed, which might have been a ready-made cats' nest. He slowly remembered where he was and with whom.

As he turned his head to see if Ruth was awake, he thought that he was in a pale mist, until he saw, first of all a cigarette, then that it was attached to her lower lip.

'Good morning, Titus.'

'Good morning, Ruth, and good morning, room.'

'How wonderful it is to be alive, to be home, even for a bit, not to be alone.'

'But you have your friends.'

'Oh, yes, they're my best friends. They know all my secrets, and what's more, they never divulge them.

They won't tell a soul you're here if you don't want them to.'

'I don't think I know a soul, but Ruth, thank you for having me, or perhaps I should say thank you for letting me stay.'

'But what else could you have done? Where could you have gone? Besides, you haven't really told me who you are.'

'Perhaps if I do, you won't believe me. There is so much to tell, so much that I almost don't want to remember, so many people I crave to see, whom I cannot. So much that I have done, and so much that I have not done. Perhaps, in time, I may be able to tell you a fraction, but I feel a tenderness for you, which is something to do with some of my past. My sister Fuchsia had a room, or rooms, something like yours. Full of love, her love. The only way she could express her abundant loving was for her things that she had collected: her books, her paintings, the flowers she picked and forgot to look after . . .'

'Titus, why don't you put your arms round me, and forget or remember with me? I believe you. I would like to enter your world. Come closer, gently and slowly. Close your eyes again.'

As Ruth's voice grew softer and her body closer, Titus felt not so much passion as tenderness, and it was with an infinite gentleness that he made love. A mutual loneliness ached through their bones, and their fulfilment ushered them back into a dreamless sleep.

They slept again for several hours, and it was the restless movement on the bed from hungry felines that woke Ruth, and a soft paw on Titus's face, which brought them back to a reality where, although they had few responsibilities, one was certainly to feed the creatures in their care, and see to all their other basic needs.

As they threw on the clothes so carelessly discarded the night before, neither felt embarrassment, but a kinship that drew them to each other.

'Well, Titus, although I am not a very practical person, one thing we can't do is to live very long without money. I'm sure that there isn't much in your pockets, and there's very little in mine. I have my emergency shelf for the moment, and I think after we've fed the cats, we'll take Dog for a walk and have some breakfast in a little place I know.'

As she was talking, Ruth climbed on to one of the tables, underneath a triangular corner shelf, and as she dislodged enough dust to cover a billiard table, there was the sound of coins being heaped together and pushed on to the table, falling and clattering like hailstones, and landing on the floor as well. She climbed off the table, pushed a strand of hair out of her eyes and left a grey track of dust from chin to forehead. Gathering up the coins and counting them, her light-heartedness returned, and with her cigarette almost dancing with excitement on her lower lip she said, 'Well, at least there's enough here for a day or two, or three or four, what's more, oh Lor', hee-haw – come on, Titus, let's go and spend it, thrift not, and then we'll talk about what you must do, and mustn't do, what you have done, and what you haven't done, because if you stay a little while with me I can help you meet some people who might give some work for some money.'

'I want to stay for a little, but you've already given me so much.'

'Let's not talk any more, but go out. Poor Dog, he's so patient and so loving and I'm so hungry now. Come on, Titus.'

The cats were fed and they left the studio, leaving the key hanging on the string, Ruth knowing that none of her possessions was of much interest to an intruder.

○ ○ ○ ○ ○

Titus saw his anchorage in daylight. The long corridor was not attractive: dark walls, where the paint had long ago flaked away, and at intervals double black doors, which opened, he assumed, on to other studios. The floor was of an undistinguishable colour, with what must have been paint stains making shapes that were not intentional. The open door through which they had passed the night before led to the steps on to the pavement, and there stood Ruth's ancient car, which they had forgotten in their tiredness to empty of its pictures and stones and branches and flowers.

They turned left down the steps and Ruth said, 'What friends I have live in these studios, but I'll take you to meet them later, after we've exhausted each other. Shall I exhaust you first, I wonder. I want to know of all the things that you have only hinted at. There is nothing I have to tell you that could in any way compete. Tell me your story soon, Titus.'

'It is not my story. It belongs to a great many others, but Ruth, you keep saying let's not talk, then talking and asking questions. It will only be in my own time that I can tell you, that is if I can, only a minute particle. It might take a lifetime and neither you nor I have time for that . . . Now let me say that I am hungry – poor Dog is hungry and you said we would have breakfast soon.'

'Of course, poor Titus, yes, it isn't far. Only about five minutes and we'll be there.'

They turned at the end of the road into a wider street that had some houses set back, with high walls and long deep windows, shuttered, rich and silent.

They walked along, past a graveyard with ancient headstones, some ivy-covered, and the names of the sleepers obliterated by time and the elements. The grass and weeds were high enough to hide some of the stones. At intervals there were wooden benches, on which sat old men and women, waiting, it seemed, to join their confrères underground, so inert and lackadaisical did they seem.

'That is a music hall,' said Ruth, and Titus mistook her remark for a rather sinister joke.

'Oh, no, not that. I mean that,' as she pointed to a red-brick building just past the graveyard. 'Perhaps we could go some time.'

As they passed this building Ruth said, 'Here we are,' and pushed open a door. It led into a little room, with stalls on each side and tables where eccentric-looking groups of people sat.

When Ruth entered, she was greeted by several of these people, with friendliness, and no curiosity at seeing her with an unknown man and his dog. 'Some time, if you like, you can meet them, but let's keep ourselves to ourselves just now, eh, Titus? Do you want to meet anyone?'

'Some time.'

'Some time, who?'

'Some time, Ruth.'

Food and hot drinks were put before them, without their asking, and a full plate for Dog was put on the floor, where he had waited so patiently.

'How nice they are here. They must know you well.'

'When I've enough money I come here every day, and they always know what I like. As you may have noticed, I am easily pleased, gastronomically, that is. Now, then, but what does "now, then", mean? Should it be then, now? How can it be now and then then, except that as soon as now is said it's then. But what I really meant to say was let's begin.'

'I like your flights of fancy. They seem to come from nowhere, but they linger in that dusty attic of my brain, and I come across them when I'm looking for something else. There, I've almost taken a leaf out of your book – why leaf, why book? Yes, let's begin.'

They both ate with pleasure, but with a certain uncon-cern for what they were eating. There was just enough to satisfy, so that they could now turn their thoughts to other matters.

'Let's go back to the studio. I have to do some work, which I will be paid for, and we can try to think what you can do.'

Ruth paid, and the three got up to leave. As they were passing the last table, the man who was sitting there called out, 'I say, fancy doing a bit of modelling?'

Titus was not sure if it were he or Ruth who was being addressed, but she said, 'This is Titus Groan. That is Herbert Drumm. He's a painter, and he's doing a mural for an old woman who only wants men in her bedroom, I mean on the walls, as she doesn't seem able to have them anywhere else. Herbert's always stopping men and asking them to pose for him *and* he pays too. What about that for your first job, eh, Titus? B Titus, you are, C Titus, you do?'

'Well, I can't say I'm the best person for standing still; in fact, I don't remember ever having done so. It's against nature, but I've never turned down a new experience. When would you like me, where would you like me and how would you like me?'

'Three good questions, old boy,' said Herbert, who was nearer sixty than fifty, with black, bushy eyebrows that were in danger of impairing his vision, a grizzled moustache and beard that made up in quantity for what was lacking on his head. His nose was rather bulbous and his complexion decidedly mottled, and the impression he gave was not so much that of a man dedicated to creative activity as of one whose search for the meaning of life lay in more bibulous pastimes. His voice was baritone, and loud, with an intonation that was rather monotonous.

'I've got to go and see the old bag now, to show her

some more of her boys, her darling boys, as she calls them. My drawings – I'll leave them with her, that'll keep her quiet, and I'll tell her about you, old boy. She likes them all, but most of all she likes the virile manly boys, like you, old boy. She has as much gold as double chins. But to get back to when, where and how, Ruth'll tell you where, I'll tell you how, and you tell me when.'

'This afternoon, then. I'll have to get into training for standing still, won't I?' said Titus.

'That's the idea, old boy, and bring your old hairy hound with you – she'll like that too, the old bag. Well, see you this afternoon.'

Titus and Ruth turned for her home, and walked back past the graveyard.

'Tell me about him,' said Titus.

'Who?' asked Ruth.

'Herbert Drumm.'

'Well, nobody knows very much about where he came from, and he's not all that helpful, but some say he was a sailor, which might be true, you'll soon see when you go to his studio and he starts to sing – but I think I'll leave that delight for you to find out for yourself.'

'I can't quite see him as a painter, though,' said Titus.

'Oh, painters aren't set in identical moulds, you'll soon see, but Mrs Sempleton-Grove thinks he looks the part.

He wears a big bow and a large-brimmed black hat when he goes to see her, and although I'd hardly say he had a rare talent, what he lacks in that respect he makes up for with a kind of almost vulgar bravura. But he's always got work, and his conscience and ethics very rarely clash. "Give 'em what they want, says I," says he, and that's just what he does.'

'And where's his studio?'

'I'll show you,' said Ruth, as they turned into the street where she lived.

Just before the steps leading up to her studio there was a stone arch, which Titus had noticed but not wondered about.

'This way,' she said. They turned and went through the archway, which led into a rather dark, very wide passage, with a black brick wall on the right, which Titus recognised as the one seen from Ruth's kitchen window. As his eyes grew used to the dark, he saw that on the left was a building or series of buildings that seemed to have been put together rather than following any sort of architectural design. They walked past these until they came to the end of the passage, which was one of the same haphazard constructions at right angles to the others. Hanging baskets of geraniums lent joyousness to the darkness. The front door was covered with brush marks and the front wall was more like a conservatory, being made of panes of glass that were painted white, to ensure a kind of privacy.

'This is where Herbert lives, where this afternoon you will enter perhaps for you a new world, although, dear Titus, I already feel that there can be very little that would surprise you. I still long to hear about your world. I feel a closeness to it that I hardly feel for this one. I am bewildered by what you have left behind to become a wanderer, a watcher, an outcast; there are few who will find themselves in sympathy with you.'

'I have felt that since I left my home. On overthrowing all that I possessed, all whom I loved or hated, I have become, as you say, an outcast. I stand by myself. I am alone, by my own action, perhaps by my own wish. I would like to stay with you for a little, but by my own nature I shall in time move on. I have hurt more people than I could ever hope to make reparation to, and although you might think it presumptuous of me, I shall hurt you, when I go, but I will hurt myself as well.'

'I know that, Titus; I've known it since I met you, but there's nothing I can do. How can anyone prevent what is ahead for us, and why should I want them to? While we can, without too much soul-searching, can't we enjoy each moment now? I feel an exhilaration that so rarely comes, and I feel capable of being buffeted and coming up again for more. But until that time we must live in the present, and you must get yourself together in a new role, as a virile man for Mrs Sempleton-Grove, via Herbert, and I must get on with my work – so let's go back now and let life drift away, becalmed, until the storms come again.'

22

Titus as Model

They walked back to Ruth's studio with Dog, who sensed Titus's affinity with her, so much so that he chose to walk by Ruth's side instead of his master's. For Titus, this indication was a good one. Despite his endeavour to have no human ties, no loves, no hates, he felt an unpossessive affection for the animal, which had displayed so much valour towards him, but he knew that when the time came he would abandon him. Perhaps Dog himself sensed it and, not sharing Titus's need for self-sufficiency, was yearning towards someone who would shield him against what was to come.

As they entered the studio the cats, according to their temperaments, remained asleep, or raised eyes and, recognising no interruption to their privacy, closed them again.

'What are you going to do then, Ruth?'

'I've got to do three drawings for a story that I don't like, and as usual they are to be done in a hurry. I've been waiting to hear if they were wanted for months and now I've heard yes, but they must be sent by the end of the month. I've got to get references and materials and, most urgent of all, my ideas straightened out or crookeded out perhaps. I might even ask you if you would pose for me some time, but I'm afraid I can't pay you! I'll have to go out now to get some special paper – so perhaps you'll have gone to Herbert's by the time I'm back, but Titus, come back, won't you. It's too soon for goodbye.'

As Ruth left to go out, Dog, without being asked, rose to follow, but she said, 'Oh, no, Dog. You've got an appointment this afternoon, but we'll be together some time – of that I am almost certain, eh, Titus?'

Titus didn't answer, for he knew the implications of Ruth's remark.

After she had left, despite the very short time Titus had known her, her absence filled the studio and Titus had a momentary wish to be like other people in wanting and needing the succour of one person, one place, a home, but he knew himself too well to think that it would ever be.

It was time to go to Herbert Drumm's, so he called Dog to him and they both went out to see what lay in store for them.

Titus found his way to Herbert's studio and knocked

on the glass panel of the door. It was opened by a lady in a black turban, dressed completely in black; her eyes were black, with deep brown shadows ringing them, which gave them a tragic appearance, and her skin was sallow with two patches of rouge flanking the hollow shadows. It might be supposed that such an appearance would be reflected in the lady's demeanour, but as she said 'Titus Groan' in a deeply accented voice, she bowed to welcome him in and her melancholy smile lent as much warmth to her personality as did the rouge to her cheeks.

She pushed forward a velvet curtain, which divided the small entrance from the main room, and invited Titus and Dog to enter.

'Ah, come in, old boy, glad to see you. Let's have a drink – bring on the booze, old girl, will you?'

The room that Titus entered was the same size and shape as Ruth's, but they were as unalike in everything else as a horse from a centaur. It seemed to have two completely different moods, not divided by anything tangible, such as a screen, but by the furnishings. There was a certain chaos where Herbert stood cleaning his brushes with turpentine, and on the other side of the room, a tidy, finicky posse of little tables with lace mats proclaimed the complete autonomy of their own domain. Titus was not able to distinguish the details of the profound difference in the two parts of the room, but he was intrigued by it.

'Sophia is my wife, old boy. She doesn't hold with painting and she likes to keep herself to herself. It's not all that easy in one room but we've reached a pretty good compromise between us, and I don't stray into her province any more than she does into mine. She came from the country, you see – anyway, let's get down to work soon. Ever done any modelling? Course you haven't – I don't know where you've come from, but you don't have to tell me, and what's more you've never stood in one place for long at a time, so I won't ask you to do too much – and old Dog – old bag Sempleton-Grove'll like him in the pic too. Thanks, old girl,' said Herbert, as Sophia strayed across the invisible dividing line of the two territories with a silver salver on which were two heavy glasses and a decanter of red wine. She put it down on a dust-covered table on which were scattered innumerable objects of so diverse a kind that Titus would not have been able, even if he had wished, to distinguish one from another.

Sophia withdrew across the frontier, without having spoken, but there was no unfriendliness in her manner and Titus took his glass of wine from Herbert as he sat down in a large armchair, whose springs were on affectionate terms with the floor.

'You are right,' he said. 'I know nothing of modelling, as you call it, and I can't see myself standing still for long, but I'd like to know how you go about what you're doing.'

'Well, we've all got our tricks, you know, old boy. I'm not much of a painter but I love the damned stuff, and I'm in luck to have got round old Sempleton-Grove – I'm slick, but I know it, and if she wants lovely boys I'll give her lovely boys, and heap them on by the basinful. No, you won't have to stand long – it's your head I want – I'll use the old bod for the rest of you,' and Herbert pointed to a life-size figure sitting in a chair, which Titus had not noticed.

'Oh, what is that?'

'That's a lay figure, old boy,' said Herbert as he went over to it and stood it up. 'It's got all its joints and there's a key for her to stay in any position I want her to . . .'

'But I'm a he,' said Titus.

'Do you know, I'm just beginning to decipher the difference between he and she, and I rather like it . . . anyway, you see, I'm only going to do some drawings of your head, and then put it on top of wonder-girl, only it'll be wonder-boy – see what I mean?'

'I think I see,' said Titus. 'I shall look forward to seeing my transformation.'

'Look, can you go on sitting in that chair, and just

keep your head as still as possible, and I'll get on with it, and your companion, that great hound, who'll be a good deal better a sitter than you.'

Titus sat with his back to the dividing line and, as he watched Herbert, was aware of the quiet rustle of movement behind him, of objects being picked up and put down, of a rattling, and a rustling and water running, and a scraping, and activity of a domestic kind that seemed ceaseless. The small domestic noises were interrupted by a huge bellow of sound from Herbert's lungs, as he raised his voice in an uninhibited song of delight. As he sang, and took great gulps at his wine, he pounced on the paper in front of him with an equal lack of inhibition; he sat in an ungainly armchair with a drawing board across his knee and, holding his thick black charcoal at arm's length, with eyes half closed, he made marks upon the paper.

'Yes, yes, keep your eyes like that, old boy – keep still for a minute – don't move, don't move – put your hand up – no, put it down, I won't be long – yes, that's it. Yes, you've got a good head – I like those hollow cheeks – it's a good nose, yes, strange eyes, yours – deep – I like that – deep set – a good nose too, you've an indefinable face – not handsome, not ugly, but a face of its own – I can't pin it down, but I'm damned well going to try – but I think you've got me there.'

As he spoke, the slight scrape of charcoal on paper conflicted with the strange domestic sounds behind Titus, which he could not always locate, but slowly and insidiously another sense was being attacked, as a most subtle aroma filled his nostrils and he became aware that he was hungry.

'Well, that's it for the time being. You can move now.'

Although Titus had made little effort to be still, he was pleased all the same to be able to move without what small conscience he had being disturbed. He stood up, he stretched his arms, he closed his eyes and breathed out, and turned his back on Herbert to look more closely at the other side of the room. He saw Sophia with an apron on, busy at a cooking stove, stirring gently at a large black pot. He had not noticed before, under the huge window, several shelves, on which stood flowering plants that showered the room with colour and life, so silently burgeoning, the very opposite of her husband's lusty, insensitive nature. Everything was loved and cared for, cleaned and orderly, in striking contrast to Herbert, whose love for his paints, his brushes, his canvas, paper, pencils and chalks was made manifest by ebullient disorder. How these two had achieved the compromise of living together and yet apart, was to Titus's mind a remarkable feat of what love or propinquity is capable of.

'I expect you'd like a rest now,' said Herbert, as he poured another glass of wine for Titus.

'Can I see what you've done?'

'Yes, old boy, but you won't see what I can see, or what I'm going to do with you.'

Titus looked at the drawings and although he knew very little, he felt a shallowness in them, a certain flair, but a vulgarity and coarseness of vision, and he didn't know what to say. Yet there was an underlying vitality.

'Yes, I know, old boy. Cheap stuff – I know. I should have stuck to the other sort of canvas. At least I know my limitations. I'm a hack, but a happy hack.'

'I don't really know much about it all, I haven't any idea, but I think it looks like me.'

'Oh, don't worry, old boy. I don't get hurt that easily. It stinks, but old Sempleton-Grove'll want to meet the model and if you're short of a coin or two and you play your cards right, she'll set you up, put you on your feet, feather your nest and all the rest of it.'

The most delicious smell began to waft across the frontier, and Titus hoped that the restrictions imposed by the dividing line were domestic, rather than culinary.

His hopes were fulfilled quite soon, as the first to be served was Dog, with a plate of meat, which he sat looking at until he was sure that his master was to be equally rewarded.

∘ ∘ ○ ∘ ∘

With a smile Sophia retraced her steps and handed Titus a silver tray, which was set to perfection with highly polished silver cutlery and cruets, a crystal glass intricately cut, a linen napkin, and a small posy of flowers, delicately arranged. He was fascinated by the incongruity of the arrangements and at the same time touched by the thoughtfulness of his hostess. He wondered if Herbert would be treated to the same amount of care and rather doubted it, until he saw him clearing a space on his dust-covered, object-laden table. The same care had been taken with the tray that was deposited on that disreputable table, and all that was now awaited was the realisation of the delicious smell into a visual presence.

'Yes, old boy, she's a wonderful woman. Funny, we don't speak the same language in any respect, but we get on. Take away my paints, my booze, my squalor, and I'd die, loud and clear. Take away her plants, her polish, her order, shining white and silver, she'd fade away, slowly and without a murmur. It's a funny way to get your satisfaction out of life, eh, old boy?'

'Yes, but I can understand it. Isn't perfection, or the pursuit of it, something to be envied?'

'You're right there, old boy. I'm a brash, haphazard old fool. I'm satisfied with outward flash – don't go deep into anything, but I'm none the less happy for that. Here it comes and I'll bet you've not tasted food like this before.'

Two plates of very fine porcelain with silver covers were put on Titus's tray, then Herbert's, and as the covers were lifted the sight as well as the smell of the food could almost have satisfied their aesthetic hunger, if it had not been for the more animal hunger that had begun to consume them, and as they started to eat so did Dog, and sitting at a linen-draped table across the border sat Sophia, straight-backed, her apron removed, and eating, with a delicate refinement, a portion a good deal smaller than her guest's.

There followed wine and dessert, and even the loquacious Herbert seemed to be silenced, until the last plate was removed, the last drop of wine drunk and Sophia had begun the task of clearing and polishing and tidying her side of the fence.

Titus was very conscious of the extreme kindness of his hostess, but was uncertain how to make his thanks known, as they seemed to have no common language, so he asked Herbert.

'Well, old boy, you just tell her in your own way and

she'll understand the gist of it. You got category A status. She likes you, that's certain.'

'I'm very grateful to your wife, and to you, but I'm not quite sure why I am so honoured.'

'Well, there's something about you, old boy. Can't say what it is, but she knows. She's got a nose (not a pun, old boy) for quality. And by the way, you haven't had your earnings yet.'

'I can hardly expect to be paid for doing nothing but sit down with my dog, and drink and eat food fit for an earl . . .'

'King, old boy, but you came here as my model and we'll stick to our plan. Anyway, it's the old bag's money. I'm going to run up these drawings into something that'll whet her appetite for you and she'll want to meet you all right. So I'll come round in a day or two to fix it. You'll be at Ruth's, will you?'

'Ruth has said I can stay as long as I like, but I never stay very long anywhere.'

'Don't you hurt her, old boy.'

'I'll try not to hurt her.'

Herbert felt in his pocket and brought out some notes, which he handed to Titus. 'Here you are, old boy – it's what we give models, so don't let's haggle.'

Titus took the money, knowing it was not deserved but feeling that he could now help Ruth a little. He rose to go and, as he rose, so Mrs Drumm came over the divide, and Titus bowed and thanked her with great courtesy for her hospitality. She smiled, with her eyes and her lips, and led him towards the door of the studio, which she opened to let him out.

23

Titus Thinks of the Past

As Titus and Dog walked back to Ruth's studio, he began to wonder if he should leave this part of his life now, before he could inflict pain on someone whom he already knew to be as vulnerable as his sister Fuchsia. Yet she had said come back, Titus, and he knew that she knew that he would go when he wanted to. Her armour was ready, but it might not be proof against the hurt when it came. Then Titus thought how arrogant it was to think that it was within his power to so dislocate a life, but from past experience he knew it to be true. He felt drawn to Ruth, already needed her, but he knew he would resist her attempt to possess him and his own willingness to be possessed.

I did promise her to return, he said to himself, thus fortifying his conscience, as he went up the steps to Ruth's studio. He knew she must be home by the sound of coughing, and as he tapped at the door, Dog gave a little whine of delight.

Ruth opened the door in a paroxysm of coughing, with the half-smoked cigarette stuck to her bottom lip.

'Oh, Titus, I'm so glad you came back. I wasn't sure – and dear Dog too. Come in, I've got the stove going, and I'm doing some work. I got the paper – it's hand-made – it's beautiful – look.'

'Yes, Ruth, it looks beautiful and, in a strange way, so do you.'

'Strangely beautiful, beautifully strange, pretty ugly, pretty pretty, plain ugly, purl and plain, a pearl of great worth, a rough diamond – thank you, Titus.'

'Have you started your work yet?'

'Well, I've got my paper, my pens, my reference books. I'm a little bit short of ideas but they'll come. They must. I've already discarded all those,' Ruth said, as she pointed to balls of paper, creased and crumpled and lying wherever she had thrown them in her dissatisfaction.

'I don't think I can help you.'

'I feel better now that you're here, Titus, and I think if you don't mind I'll get back to work now, but first of all tell me how you got on at Herbert's.'

Titus told Ruth of his first venture into modelling, which seemed to consist mainly of sitting down, eating and drinking.

'Oh, they're so kind, those two,' said Ruth. 'I expect

Herbert will take you to meet Mrs Sempleton-Grove later. But Titus . . . beware.'

'I've met many rich women before, and there is a common denominator . . .'

'Common?'

'Well, uncommon, then, but all right, what shall I say? I've never met a rich woman who suffers from an inferiority complex, or who doesn't feel that all she possesses is hers by some undefined right, including the right to possess her latest lover until she tires of him . . .'

'I really want to get on now, Titus. I'm quite sure you'll know what to do with Mrs Sempleton-Grove, so I shan't worry. Are you staying, or going out?'

'I thought I'd leave you in peace and look around to see what I can see. Do you want to come out, Dog?'

Dog had been lying near Ruth's work table and he stood up as Titus spoke to him, but remained in the same place.

Titus said, 'Well, I'm going now, aren't you coming?'

Dog walked slowly to the door, as Titus opened it, but made no move to follow him. He acted as any host might behave to his guest and waited courteously until that guest had completely taken his leave, before closing the door, in this case, with a large soft paw.

When Titus left the studio he felt isolated, more lonely

than was his wont. The walls of his heart had been breached. He had thought he was immune, a nature not subject to human feeling. But why? he asked himself. Because I am different. I belong to a past that I have rejected. I am a pariah. Why am I to exist without human contact? Why do I feel that I may inflict pain without retribution? Since Juno I have learned that there is something in me that can hurt but I have also been damaged by that waif, that being of gossamer, that 'Thing'. The sprite, the cruel piece of nature, who taunted me has killed whatever tenderness I might have shared with another. My heart breaks when I think of Fuchsia, and the staunch, beautiful, ageing Juno. Ruth, too, is a woman who will give until she dies . . . So thought Titus as he wandered towards the river. It was the first time that he had been without Dog and he missed him. He walked on the dark pavements, not knowing where he was going; he let his footsteps guide him, down darkened roads, looking through lit windows at people unaware of those outside looking in, who were gathered in family groups, or couples in an embrace that only time could force apart.

He went in through one door, drawn by the sound of hilarity, the only explanation being drink. He was not a great drinker, but in the mood he was in, human company impelled him to push open the door.

The noise, and the fumes of drink and smoke, were enough to swamp his need for human contact, and he was backing out as a woman lurched forward and with a hoarse and vulgar hiccup clutched at his arm. 'Oh, sorry, darling,' she said, peering at him with eyes that saw nothing, they were so glazed. All Titus could see was the demarcation line where her raven hair changed from black to white.

'You're just in time,' she said.

Titus said nothing as she propelled him into the room to a bar, where people were propped up in varying degrees of inebriation.

'In time for what?' asked Titus.

'Well, tha' depends, what you mean by time – eh, wha'? Wha' abow a drink . . . eh? Tha's wha' ah meant – time to gi' me a drink.'

Titus was in no mood for banter, for drinking, for compassion towards a middle-aged woman's maudlin attentions, so that with a little of the money he had earned that afternoon he bought her a drink, and the haze of smoke was so thick, both in the bar and her brain, that he made his way out. His mood of introspection and lack of love for the human race was not acceler-ated by this little episode, but it was good for him to be alone and free from pursuit of any kind. In the back of his mind he suffered an ache of conscience for what he knew he was going to do to Ruth, yet he knew that he was powerless to prevent himself.

It was getting dark as he crossed the wide road that led to the embankment, and he made his way to the wall, where he stood listening to the lapping of the water, a sound that filled him with a nostalgia that had no reason, but for the melancholy with which it filled him. One or two barges drifted by in the darkness, and he felt out of his element and anxious, and as he heard the water his mind went back to the distant sounds and sights of a flood which, if it had not happened sooner, was to turn him from youth to manhood by the taking of a life so malignant that to him it was an act of bene-faction. The ache of longing to see his sister Fuchsia was unbearable. He could not and never would be able to associate her with death, whose life had been so short and unfulfilled. In thinking of Fuchsia, his mind returned to the present, to Ruth, whose vulnerability was parallel to his sister's. He turned and made his way back to the studio.

24

Moments of Serenity

As Titus walked back through the darkened streets, he longed to give something to Ruth, which would expiate the hurt that he knew he was going to inflict on her. But of material things there was nothing that she would wish for, even if he had the power or the money to buy them. I have only myself, and in my own eyes that is of doubtful value, we both know, he thought. He passed a house that was withdrawn from the road by a deep laurel hedge and a holly tree. Even in the gloom he could see it was loaded with bright berries. He stopped under the street lamp and cut a branch.

The leaves pricked his fingers as he carried it, and as he went up the steps to the studio he cradled it against his chest. He had to grope along the unlit corridor until he came to the door and, although there was no sound, there was a glimmer of light, so that he did not put his hand through the letterbox to withdraw the key, but tapped on it gently.

He heard the sound of footsteps and the softer patter of canine pads before the door was opened, then the wheezing cough of a smoker.

'Oh, Titus, I'm so glad to see you.' Dog, standing beside Ruth as a huge ochre-coloured protector, gave a whimper of welcome and backed to let him in.

The room was almost overheated by the big, black, living monster of a stove, and a light on the table revealed a disorder of paper and pens, pencils, ink and all the paraphernalia of an artist at work, topped by a cat or two sitting on small mountains of books and paper.

'What a beautiful sight, Ruth,' Titus could not help exclaiming. 'How have you managed? Is it going better now? Your drawing, I mean.'

'Well, yes. Yes and no – I'm disturbed, and sometimes that's better. Sometimes not. When I'm disturbed, some-times I work better if I've had a few drinks. Sometimes, then, it clears my mind and so long as I can control my pen or my brush, I can turn out the dross and see clearly what I want to do. I'm happy – unhappy – exhilarated, despairing, desperate, hopeful – lost, and found.'

'Yes, Ruth, I can feel all these things, and without arrogance too. I had to come back, to see you, to feel your warmth, but I dreaded it too.'

'Oh, I know that, Titus. But what can we do – eh? I *know*. I expect you could do with something to eat. How practical I am, eh? Come on, let's pretend. Come on, Titus. Come in. Let's pretend there is no world outside, back or beyond, past or future. Just *now*. Come on. I can't work any more anyway. Come on. Come on. Let's eat a little, drink a little more and grasp what we can . . .'

'I've brought you something,' said Titus, and he handed Ruth the holly branch, which she took, acknowledging what lay beyond the gift. 'It's rather prickly,' he warned her.

'Prickles, stickles, red and green, look out, look out, my lily queen,' chanted Ruth as she laid it on the overburdened table, and one cat, on being so unceremoniously displaced, jumped off the paper mountain.

Ruth lit the candles in the black three-pronged candle holder and motioned Titus to a dilapidated magenta armchair, which sat guard by the stove.

'I'll bring the soup in, and then let's see what happens. I'm tired, hungry, I want to dance, to sing, to weep, to laugh, to sleep, to wake. Come on, Titus, what do you want to do?'

'I just want to be here. I feel safe.'

Ruth left the room and Dog stayed, not knowing now whether to stay or go. He stayed in the centre of the studio, and Titus and his canine friend heard the sounds from across the corridor of crockery being moved, put down and lifted, and clatter, clatter, down she came again, kicked open the door and brought in a tray, on which stood a saucepan, steaming, and plates and two glasses and a bottle of wine.

Titus got out of his chair and, taking the tray, deposited it on the floor.

'I must give them all something first, then we can settle down and see what we shall see – eh, Titus Groan?'

Ruth put down plates of food for the cats, and a larger bowl for Dog, who with his customary courtesy made no move until he saw that his master and his hostess were also served.

Ruth sat in another chair on the other side of the stove, and in the candlelit silence, with candlelit thoughts, they all settled down to eat and drink what had been prepared.

'I'm tired, Titus. Will you take Dog out now, for a bit. The cats have their own private door but poor Dog, he can't get through that.'

They stacked up the plates and bowls, and Ruth told Titus to leave it on the floor, just where it was.

'Yes, I'll take Dog.'

'Leave the door open, Titus. I expect I'll be in bed when you get back.'

Titus groped his way back along the corridor to the front door of the building, which was never closed.

When he returned the candles were still lit, and he saw Ruth's dark head on the pillow, with the little drift of smoke coming from the cigarette, clinging as always to her lower lip.

As she removed it, the wheezing cough reached the proportions of a small dust storm, and her laughter fought the wheezing until the bed shook and the cats were displaced in a most inelegant way.

Titus threw off his clothes and dropped them beside the bed, with no attempt to arrange them, and as Ruth removed the cigarette, she slid to the side of the bed against the wall and Titus, with the sigh of coming home, lay down beside her.

They slept deeply and innocently. It was only in the early hours of the morning that they awoke and their lovemaking was half in another world, so that on waking at dawn neither knew if they had dreamed it. It was then that Titus opened his heart to Ruth. It was then that for hours he talked of his childhood, of the home he had forsaken, the people he had loved and hated. The landscape – the castle – all that it stood for – all that at times he could hardly breathe for the longing for, and the hatred of. Ruth listened as he spoke, shed tears for the death of Fuchsia, ached for Keda, and was silenced in her tears for that being, to whom Titus would be for ever bound – the 'Thing', amoral, beautiful and heartless. She took it all to her heart. She wanted to return with Titus to the few who remained. His mother, the magnificent Gertrude, whose russet hair must by now surely have turned to the colour of flint. She clung to Titus, with a love that almost broke her and realised that nothing and no one could hold a wandering man. She had no doubts. Her acceptance of him was absolute.

Ruth knew that, whatever happened, whether sooner or later, she would be for ever, like Titus, alone. But she would not have had it otherwise, and she prepared herself anew for the wounds to come.

For many days they lived in the studio. Ruth working, Titus going out and returning, and savouring a life they knew could not last. They hardly spoke. There was no need. Both wondered where, when and how the world would intrude.

One morning there was a hearty rapping on the door and Herbert's voice called, 'Ripe strawberries – ripe strawberries – anyone there? Ripe strawberries – you there, old boy, ripe strawberries.'

Ruth looked at Titus, as she went to open the door, and Herbert came in with his arms full of what looked like a harvest festival.

'Sophia sent you these, old girl,' and he put down,

where he could find a place, a pie dish with a crust of golden pastry, and as much fruit and vegetables as his hands could hold.

'Oh, how kind of her,' said Ruth. 'My mouth waters, for I've tasted her cooking and it's memorable – do please thank her – how wonderful. I'm afraid my prowess stops at a bowl of soup and some bread.'

'Well, old boy, it's as I thought – I've dolled up the drawings of you and the old bag won't rest until I've taken you to see her. Can you come now, with me? She's worse than I am when she gets an idea in her head, and it's always got to be done NOW, no matter what anyone else's plans are. Can you come, old boy, eh?'

Titus looked at Ruth, and he knew she felt a shrinking of her heart.

'Well, I'm not . . .'

'Oh, yes, Titus, do go. I've got so much to get on with. I must finish these drawings. I have to take them up tomorrow. They've promised to pay me on the dot . . . and carry one.'

'Good girl,' roared Herbert. 'Oh, she's a good girl.'

'What about Dog?' asked Titus.

'Well, the old bag's keen on virility and all that, but I think one specimen at a time, old boy.'

'I'll keep him, Titus, while you're out.'

'Oh, good girl, that's the girl. Come on, Tite, old boy.

You never know what might happen once you get through old Sempleton's portals. Let's get going – we can walk there.'

'All right, I'll follow you then. I just want a word with Ruth before I go.'

'Don't worry, old fellow. I know where I'm not wanted. I'll wait for you by the front door.'

Herbert burst into an arpeggio of song as he bashed his way noisily out of the studio door.

'Is that all right, Ruth? Do you mind my going?'

'Of course not, Titus.'

'You know, Ruth . . .'

'Yes, I know.'

'I will be back.'

'Of course, Titus . . . goodbye, then, or more appropriately, goodbye now.'

Titus gently kissed her, and as he left the studio Dog went back to Ruth and pushed his muzzle into her lowered face.

25

At Mrs Sempleton-Grove's

Titus joined Herbert on the outside steps and they made their way down quiet side roads, past rather mean little terraced houses with blankets at windows, and broken panes of glass, peeling paint and neglected children looking out. From these dreary houses they turned at the end of the road and the whole house-scape changed to an elegance of white-painted houses, each front door painted a different colour and window boxes, a fantasy of colour and plant, set off like jewels by the whiteness of the bricks. An orderly world, at least from the outside, beautiful and cared for.

'Well, it's not far, old boy. I don't think I'll stay long – she won't care anyway. She doesn't fancy me – I'm a bit old hat – long in the tooth or what have you, but she'll be an experience anyway.'

'I've met many rich women, you know.'

'I dare say you have, old boy. Still you never know, you never know.'

They made their way down a cul-de-sac, which was bounded by a very large four-storeyed house with an imposing portico and steps leading up to the front door, wrought-iron grilles at the windows, and a brass door knocker shaped like a tropical fish.

'Here we are, old boy,' said Herbert, as he tugged at the bell-pull, which sounded on the other side of the door with an imperiousness worthy of a dowager.

The door was opened by a youngish dark man, dressed in black tights and a black leather jacket. He was small and lithe, with the body of a dancer, and possessed what Titus thought was a rather withdrawn dignity, until he spoke, and his voice was high, thin and nasal.

'This is Henry, Titus,' said Herbert.

'She's expecting you,' said Henry, with a rather unpleasant leer. 'Go on up, 'erbert'll take you. I've 'ad 'er malarkin' about all day – spent the morning looking for a dress, upstairs, downstairs, in and out the window, she accused me of pinching it, as near as. Two hours, I was, lookin' for the thing, and then you know what? She'd got it on all the time. I said to 'er, I've got better things to do than go looking all the morning for a dress you're wearin', but she said she thinks she's in love. Well, you've a treat in store, Titus, and no mistake.'

Saying this, Henry did a little pirouette and a twist

and a turn and, with an elegant gesture of his hands, pointed the way upstairs.

The hall was pale, the carpet was pale. The walls had alcoves in which were dark paintings, ornately framed. Huge vases of flowers, a spinet and a harpsichord, and delicate small tables of rosewood were scattered with consummate taste, and a lack of anyone loving or caring for them. A museum of taste and money, but no home.

A curved carpeted staircase with wrought-iron banisters led upstairs, and Herbert, whose exuberance seemed to have disappeared, led Titus up the staircase to the third door, on which he knocked.

A rather husky-dusky voice was heard. Whatever it said was not intelligible, but obviously enough for Herbert to obey its order.

He pushed open the door. The house seemed full of silence.

'Come in, Titus,' he said, in a voice so subdued that it was not recognisable.

They entered a very large room with four windows of excellent proportions which reached from floor to ceiling. This room was also full of furniture of great beauty and rarity.

The husky voice spoke again and at first Titus couldn't make out where it came from. At the far end of the room was an enormous painted screen, which almost made another room, and Titus traced the voice to behind the screen.

Herbert led him over, then said, 'I've brought Titus Groan to see you,' and gently pushed Titus behind the screen.

Propped up on an ornate chaise longue, shaped rather like a royal barge, was Mrs Sempleton-Grove, with her feet crossed.

Titus saw a woman whose beauty seemed to be draining away almost by the minute. He thought she was about seventy years old, with bright yellow hair dragged back into a ponytail and little curls arranged with disorder on her forehead, and drifting like gossamer around her ears. Black eyelashes of an inordinate length and thickness fluttered as she lifted her eyes (which were of a surprisingly pale blue) to Titus. She didn't speak, but gestured to him to sit on a frail gold chair that stood at the end of the chaise longue. She took no notice whatsoever of Herbert, who, with all personality dead as the bee when its sting has gone, drifted out of the room as silently as a priest reading his breviary. Titus sat without speaking and looked at his hostess more closely. She was dressed most inappropriately in what looked like a little girl's pink blouse with big puffed sleeves and incongruously she picked up a large pair of knitting needles and began to knit with what Titus could only think was more show than expertise.

'Well . . . I'm in love, you see,' said Mrs Sempleton-Grove, or that is what Titus thought had been said, for her voice was husky and slurred, as though from drugs or drink.

'Ring the bell, Titus.'

Titus looked around for a bell and found one at the side of the marble mantelpiece. He walked to the other end of the room and pushed the bell. He heard no sound, but his quick perception obviously satisfied Mrs Sempleton-Grove, for she made no remark as he regained his frail golden chair.

'Oh, do give me my reticule,' she said, pointing to a large oblong bag of gros point, which lay by her feet at the end of the chaise longue. As he handed it to her she let fall her ponytail, and her rather sparse hair drifted untidily around her face, not adding to the youthfulness that was being so desperately nurtured. She sought in her reticule and after a few moments of objects being stirred round and round as though they were ingredients of a stew, she brought forth a small hairbrush, a large comb, blue ribbon and a silver hand mirror.

Titus watched, as he had watched other women of all

ages and degrees of beauty. Mrs Sempleton-Grove brushed her lacklustre hair and pulled it into two bunches on either side of her face, and round each bunch she tied a blue ribbon, which might have been entrancing on a small girl.

As she finished, the door opened and a trolley appeared, rattling cups and plates. Henry manoeuvred it with evident distaste, rather as some men might on having to steer a pram containing their offspring reluctantly past their erstwhile drinking companions.

'Don't say thank you, then,' he said, as he left the trolley, becalmed, by Titus's side, and with a pout went to the door. Before closing it completely he put his head round the corner and stuck his tongue out.

'Do pour the tea, Titus, and I'll have some of that chocolate cake, and can you bring that cushion and put it behind my back too.'

Titus did all these things. It didn't worry him in the least. Spoiled women were usually rapacious in their demands, particularly if they wanted something in return.

She didn't suggest he should have some tea, or cake, but sat silently sipping and eating her own.

'Herbert tells me you might sit for me.' At least that is how Titus interpreted the rather blurred sentence addressed to him.

He really couldn't be bothered to say yes or no, or why or when, so he stayed silent, which did not discomfort Mrs Sempleton-Grove at all.

'After tea, I will show you my paintings.'

Titus had not known his hostess for more than half an hour but he was already managing to translate her muffled rather inconsequential conversation into intelligibility.

'Thank you, Titus,' she said as she handed him her cup and plate, which he took and replaced on the trolley. She held her hand out to him to help her off her chaise longue, then stood a little shakily by his side. As she turned, he noticed that her blouse, at the back, did not meet where the buttons should be, but was held together by one safety pin attached to another, until they met at the opposite edge where the buttonholes were, rather like a hastily constructed bridge. She was of moderate height, and as she walked further into the room Titus saw that she had the slim legs of a girl.

She went out of the large drawing room and walked along the corridor to another door. Titus followed her, assuming that that was to be his role.

The room they entered was very different from the elegant drawing room. It had the trappings of comfort: a thick carpet, warmth, and all the ease of a dilettante studio, compared to the working-living studio of Ruth's.

Magnificent easels and equipment, Titus imagined, for the many media an artist might turn to, and all of finest quality. On the walls were framed paintings, leaving little space between. Titus knew very little about painting, but enough to realise that the paintings on the walls were slight.

'I'm a bad painter. Yes, I know you think so too. But I love painting, Titus. You are blaming me for having all these things, while real painters can't afford them. Don't judge me too soon. Even if I'd been poor, I'd have been a bad painter, but at least I'm a bad painter on good materials, and I know a good painter when I see one. Herbert is worse than I am, but he has to paint to live, so there you are. I'll show you his murals in a minute.'

Titus realised there was very little need for him to speak, or even to listen, but despite any preconceived notion he might have formed of Mrs Sempleton-Grove as a rich spoiled woman, he felt it was wrong to do so. There was a kindness in her, and he felt he had little enough to be proud of in his own behaviour towards people to start judging others.

She led Titus out of her painting room up a small flight of stairs and into a room that in earlier days might have housed servants. Even so, its proportions were elegant, but what had been made of it was less so. The background colour was white, and the murals that enclosed the room, and made it rather claustrophobic, were crudely painted. Mainly figurative, and depicting men, all young, all handsome in their different way. Titus recognised Henry in some of them, in various dancing postures.

'Herbert thinks this is what I want, you know, Titus. He's done some drawings of you – that's why I wanted to meet you. He can get a likeness, but he's crude. Only it was because I thought you looked like a man that I wanted to see you. The only men I see now aren't. The trouble is I can see myself as I really am, and it doesn't make getting through the day any easier. I know I make myself into a freak. I'm trying to stay young, and the more I do, the more ludicrous I look, but I won't give up. Once, when I went into a room, everyone looked at me, but it wasn't to laugh. Every day was an adventure. I had an ulterior motive in getting Herbert to bring you here, but having met you, I know just how wrong I was. Whoever you are, you wouldn't rise to my bait. I'm surrounded by Henrys. They come and they go, and they take all they can while they can. Not that I'm easy. I can make life hell for them and they don't stay long, just long enough for us to hate each other, despise each other, then another Henry comes. How would you feel about staying for a little while? You won't have to do anything of any sort.'

'I'm not really someone who stays anywhere long, you know,' said Titus, almost the first sentence he had spoken since coming to Mrs Sempleton-Grove's.

'My dear Titus, I had already realised that. That's what makes you so attractive. All the same, won't you let me do a painting of you? Apart from everything else it will make Henry so annoyed. He must fancy you himself. I know he put his tongue out at me when he left the room. He always does, and he thinks I don't know. There have been so many Henrys. He'll go when he's got all he thinks he can get out of me. The trouble is I know it all, but they're the only kind of people who'll put up with me. I don't like being alone. It makes me think too much. Even if I'd been ten or twenty years younger, I couldn't have seduced you. When I was a girl a middle-aged man said he loved me for what I would become, and now I'm awaiting a young man who will fall in love with me for what I was!'

Titus remained silent.

'You beast. I won't say goodbye, then.'

26

From Riches to Rags

As he left the house, Titus thought of returning at once to Ruth. The pull of her warmth and love was almost bitter to him. It denied the strength of the defences he had been building for so long against any skirmishing in the region of his heart. The bastion could fall, and rebuilding would take more courage than he felt he was capable of. He averted his mind from Ruth awaiting him. He averted his mind from Dog. He could not think of the future, or of the past. The present was blank, because that was what he wanted.

Walking away from Mrs Sempleton-Grove's house Titus let this blankness lead him. He was not really aware of the physical aspect of the streets along which he walked, the people he passed, the light diminishing, the sounds, the constant noise of traffic, a city noise, impersonal but buzzing in his head.

He walked for several hours, still unaware of the changing townscape through which he passed. It was dark by now, and he became conscious of a small hunger. In his pocket there were a few coins left from Herbert's money and, as he came to from his blankness, he found he was standing outside a derelict house, in a street that offered little of comfort to anyone. It was only dimly lit, but Titus could see the decay of what once must have been a row of superbly proportioned houses, and he thought of his late hostess. The carcasses still had a little flesh on them and the rafters of the roof displayed themselves as cleanly picked as any animal left to the mercy of a vulture.

Toothless windows, and doors ajar on to a murky, dangerous emptiness. It took a little time for a sound to penetrate Titus's hearing. It was not a pleasant sound, and as he became more conscious of it he distinguished rough voices, which were raised from time to time in violent dispute – blurred, whining, ugly. He was startled by the wrenching open of a door, a shrill voice, and a missile that had accompanied the voice narrowly missing his head and breaking into fragments at his feet. A dark shape followed, tottering up from what must have been the basement of the house, and walking unsteadily along the path that separated the house from the pavement. It drew nearer to Titus, who felt no fear but a certain curiosity.

'An don' yer com back wivout it, you dirty bastard . . .'

The figure nearly tripped on the uneven paving stones and put out its hands to steady itself. It touched Titus's hand, which had involuntarily stretched out to protect whatever or whoever was having so much difficulty in standing upright.

He heard a deep booming ejaculation, like a foghorn in the mist, just as eerie and portentous a sound: 'Look where yer bleedin' goin'.'

'Sorry, I was in the way,' was all that Titus could think of saying.

''Ere, got any money?'

Titus was able to see a little, in the dim street, of what this newfound companion looked like. He was small and thickset. His clothes were layered, one on top of the other, coats and jackets, and tied up with string. There was not quite enough light to see the face under the battered hat.

'The name's Mick. If I don' get back wiv it, they'll blow me brains out. Wha's yer name?'

'Titus.'

'Blimey. Come on.'

Titus went where he was being pushed. As they walked, each in his different way, one fairly firm, the other cursing whenever he tripped, a stale smell began to envelop Titus, rank and thick, but sickly sweet at the same time. Mick cleared his throat and spat, Titus retched and turned away to ward off the appalling fumes.

'I know. I stink. That's why no woman'll look at me.'

By holding his breath and keeping his mouth closed, Titus avoided the physical result of nausea, but he dared not speak, even if he had wanted to.

They reached the end of the road and came to another, very wide, very deserted and even more decayed and hopeless than the one where this encounter had begun.

Titus felt his hand being grabbed, 'Give it us.'

He put his hand in his pocket and brought out most of the coins, which he put into Mick's mittened hand.

'Stay 'ere.'

Titus stayed. He heard voices, disputing, and the whining, cajoling tones of his friend. Then the door was pushed open and out he came, his pockets bulging and holding to his mouth a huge bottle from which he was draining as much as he could in as little time as possible, spilling what he couldn't get down on to his outer coverings, to add to his malodour.

They walked back the way they had come, until they reached the house from whose bowels Mick had emerged.

'Comin' in?'

'For a bit,' answered Titus, as they groped their way

down steps, which in earlier times would have led to an ordered world of pots and pans of burnished copper.

Mick gave three taps on a broken window and a low little whistle, then turned to Titus to gesture him to follow. One candle lit a scene, which could be called nothing if not squalid. The smell so thick that Titus felt it was tangible. Two hands grabbed at the pockets of the vagrant's clothes, and it was luck only that saved the bottles from breaking, as they were pulled unceremoni-ously towards them, the man with them.

Ugly oaths were shouted, and two figures collapsed on the floor, seemingly all acrimony spent for the time being, as the silence was broken only by the gulps and belches of some need being mercifully satisfied.

In the corner of the once-room was a mound, a stack of newspapers that moved slightly, the paper rattling, but not crisply as an unread one. Nothing in this hole could be crisp, and it was only because of the pig-like grunts coming from under the paper that Titus knew there was something alive there.

The candle allowed a stranger no great glimpse into the secrets it was hiding in all but the small area it lit up, but what Titus could see were the remains of a kitchen dresser, from floor to ceiling, with drawers hanging open and empty spaces where other drawers had been. He could only make out what he thought were one or two broken cups.

Mick had escaped into his own private oblivion. The pile of newspaper on the floor crackled more urgently and a head appeared. The head was covered by some kind of woollen hat, but Titus thought it was a female head and when it spoke the tone was not rough or coarse. There was an elegance of speech in it, which pierced his imagination.

His mind went over the nature of those who had left the organised world for the anarchic; both male and female who belonged nowhere, whose choice was made for myriad reasons. He felt at one with them, despite the squalor and poverty. He recoiled from the stench but understood the freedom the dark basement offered where layers of ordered life were peeled away.

From the not quite crisp crackling of newspapers a thin hand emerged, stretching out for benison. The grimy nails and the blue veins appeared like tributaries, and the cultured voice called for anaesthetic. No help came from the inmates of this dank region; each one was isolated in his own realm. Titus wrenched the bloated bottle from Mick and transferred it to that skinny hand, which grabbed it, and gulped and gulped to drown reality.

Titus took the only candle, to discover for himself

the nature of the face behind the hand. He held it close and saw two dead eyes, a fine nose, and lips which, when the bottle had been drained, opened on to the black cavern of teeth, little stumps of broken blackness, like the old tarred wooden posts of a forgotten beach breakwater. What he was looking at had once been a woman. As he decided to leave these remnants, he heard steps descending, and a light flashed across the room with the abruptness of the moon emerging from behind clouds. Suddenly voices broke the silence. The dark humps of humanity were being bundled out of the basement, up the squalid litter-thick steps. Titus felt himself being manhandled, pushed up the steps, out of the gate and into the waiting car.

27

Other Places, Other Work

Titus was pushed beside Mick into the back of the car. There was no dissent. It must all have happened many times before but they were too old to be saved or indoctrinated. All that could be done was to move them from one place to another until their hearts gave out, their lungs collapsed, their spirits drowned and their eyes closed for the last time, but that was not quite yet.

Desultory voices spoke in the front of the car, until it stopped, then the pantomime recommenced. The clowns were pushed and shoved, and Titus with them. They found themselves in a brightly lit official room. The remnants were marked off and taken away.

'Your name?'

'Titus Groan.'

'Not seen you before – occupation?'

'Traveller.'

'Vagrant?'

'Means of support?'

Titus reached in his pocket and found the few remaining coins, which he put on the counter in front of him.

'I see. A man of property!'

What was the point of speaking?

'Take him away.'

He was led into a small room. The key turned in the lock.

He was exhausted and hungry, and too much of each to care for any other sensation. He fell into a thick, dark sleep. When he awakened his limbs ached and he stretched himself with the abandon of a cat. He could not think where he was. He closed his eyes and was startled to hear a voice, which came from above him.

'Hello,' it said.

He rubbed his eyes and his face, then tried to trace the sound. Light came from a tiny window above his head, and he began to try to read his surroundings like a map that was unfamiliar to him.

'Well, hello then,' it said again.

Titus remembered the events of the previous evening. He found himself on a hard mattress. He saw a barred door and uninviting walls of dun-coloured brick. He put his arm up and it met some iron slats, and as he raised his head, he saw a head leaning down towards him. It had a smile. It had a gingery-white beard. He could take in no more detail but that there was no animosity towards him.

'Well, well. We're in the same boat, then. What are you on, then? Drunk and disorderly, that's me. Funny that. I'm an orderly you know. That's why I'm drunk. Couldn't take it. Had to get away for a bit. They'll let me out now. They know me. Doesn't happen often. I want to get back, but sometimes I go round the bend, like the lot of them. Anyway, sorry to talk so much. Can I help you? Anyway, what's your name? What do you do?'

'Titus.'

'Titus?'

'Yes. Titus Groan.'

'Oh, well – I'm Peregrine Smith. Why are you here?'

'No reason, really. I just ran into a basement, and I was prodded out of it.'

'Oh, I know, Mick and his friends. I'll help you. Do you want a job? That'll do the job. We want a ward orderly. We want more, as many as we can get. Are you afraid? Had any experience?'

'I'm not afraid, but it's difficult to be afraid before I know what to be afraid of.'

'A man after my own heart. I'll tell them you're with me and were merely trying to help the old friends. They'll just want to make sure someone will speak for you. I'm going back this afternoon. You can come too.

They'll be only too glad to have you. I'll vouch for you. Breakfast'll be here soon. You hungry?'

'I'm hungry – I'm dirty – I'm thirsty.'

'Well, we'll have a clean-up and then we'll get going. There's the wherewithal here,' said Peregrine as he let himself down from the bunk above Titus's head and pointed to the elementary articles of hygiene.

Ablutions and formalities completed, Titus and his newfound protector took their leave of their night's jailers, and went out into the wide empty streets, where the rough wind was not blowing poetically through a field of corn, but was playfully toying with the sordid litter of an unlovely urban purgatory.

'First, I suggest a breakfast fit for us, if not the gods. What do you say to that, Titus? Then we can get the coach. It takes us to outside the gates.'

The coach took them through the outskirts of the town, until it came to rather barren heathland.

'It won't be long now. If you look over there you'll see the towers; we get off at the end of the drive. If we're lucky there may be a staff car we can get a lift in. Otherwise it's a good old walk.'

Titus looked across the heath and in the distance, partly hidden by trees, he saw gaunt and rather forbidding black towers, which gave him no sense of eagerness to know the place better.

Several people got off the coach at the same time as Titus and Peregrine, who acknowledged them by name. Walking forward a few yards they came to heavy iron gates, which were closed, but at their side was a gate through which they went. A porter's lodge was on the inside, and a rather surly little wizened man asked for their papers.

Peregrine showed his papers, then motioned to Titus saying that he was coming to help in the wards.

'Can't take any responsibility for who you bring here, Smith.'

'That's all right, Tom. I'll answer for him.'

'If you say so – get on in.'

It was dusk by now, and the huge building in front of them was gradually being lit, which seemed to accentuate rather than diminish its formidable aspect; it was massive, aloof and rich in turrets.

Peregrine and Titus made their way through a large box hedge until they came to a side door, through which Peregrine ushered his companion. A gloomy yellow globe of light overhead did not conceal the archaic and ugly flaking walls of ochre, painted many years earlier.

'We'll go to the common room, then I'll have a word with the super and I'll fix you up with a room. Do you feel like starting work tomorrow, Titus?'

'Yes, but I'd like to know a bit about what I'm to do.'

'Oh, yes, I'll initiate you – I'm the ward nurse on Ward 12 and I'll keep an eye on you. Mind you, I can't say you may not be a bit upset by it all, but I've got quite fond of some of them, though there are others – oh, lord, yes. It can be difficult, and they can be . . . you need your patience, and your humour, and your compassion, and your strength, and above all leave your mind alone, or you might find yourself an inmate too.'

Titus found himself in unfamiliar surroundings yet again. He let himself be led into them with his eyes open.

28

Among the Dead Men

Titus awoke early in a rather drab little room and for a moment had no idea where he was. Slowly he remembered the various events of the last few days, and he wondered what now lay in store for him. There was a tap on the door.

Peregrine entered the room. He was dressed in a white overall, and over his arm there was a second one. In his other hand he held a mug of steaming liquid.

'Here you are, Titus. When you're dressed, put this overall on, and we'll go and have breakfast; then I'll take you to the super and show you the ward. I'll be back in ten minutes.'

Titus dressed. It did not take him long, as his clothes were scanty. He drank the hot tea and put on his white robe of office, and as he finished it another tap came on the door and Peregrine entered once again.

They went down several flights of stone stairs, their shoes signalling their descent with an echoing clatter,

until they came to a vast hallway, with a skylight illumi-
nating it, to its great disadvantage.

On both sides of the hall were double glass doors
and Peregrine turned right when they reached the
bottom of the stairs. Titus followed him as he pushed
open the glass door, and was amazed to see a corridor
that stretched endlessly from where they stood to the
horizon. As they began to walk down it, their footsteps
once again striking the stone floor like knells of doom,
desultory figures appeared, seemingly going nowhere.
Some turned into doorways on the left of the corridor;
they knocked, and after some seconds and a sound of
keys jangling, the disconsolate figures would disappear
behind the door, and the grating of keys in locks could
be heard again.

There was a common denominator in the people
who passed Titus and Peregrine. Of all shapes and sizes,
of both sexes and all ages, yet their gazes were turned
inward. They did not see where they were, or who was
there. Some sloped, some dragged their feet, some
shuffled, some almost ran, some would take a few paces,
then stand still, looking but not seeing. Some were
holding irate conversations with themselves; others
shouted obscenities. There was an anarchic lack of order,
but Titus reflected that in the world outside these thick
walls he had seen people behaving in the selfsame way.

That he was in a hospital for people who were mentally disturbed he knew, but of the scores of people whom he had met in his wanderings there were few whose strange quirks would not have qualified them for a place in this institution. He pondered, what is sanity, what is normal? He was unable to reach any conclusion: the immediate present called for something other than intellectual activity. In fact, as he was to learn, it was better to suspend that side of himself in favour of preserving unlimited physical strength and as much imaginative insight as possible. These thoughts were passing through Titus's mind as he walked the endless corridor.

At the end of the corridor Peregrine said, 'Well, here we are, Ward 12' and as he spoke he took out a large bunch of keys and, fitting one into the lock, pushed open the door. The first thing Titus noticed was the smell. It reminded him a little of the stench that had permeated the cellar where he had met Mick and his fellow vagrants. It was sickly and heavy and, although he had a strong constitution, his stomach turned.

'I'll take you to meet the super first. A few formalities, you know. We don't want any trouble from the others. Just casual work, yours. They're a bit touchy.'

Behind the locked door were screens that hid most of the interior of the large room, so that Titus could not see, only smell, where he was to work. Peregrine ushered him into a small office, cluttered with papers, timetables on the walls, a desk at which a rather anonymous white-coated man sat. He acknowledged the two men with an unsmiling nod and made no effort to put them at their ease.

'This is Titus Groan. He is a traveller. He's willing to help out at the moment for a few weeks. There'll be no trouble from him, I'll vouch for that. What d'you say?'

'Any experience?'

'A great deal,' answered Titus, with a truth that was not quite to the point.

'We could do with another pair of hands, there are three off now. We'll take you on for a stated time, with conditions. If you break them, out you go.'

Titus was given conditions that restrained him from any kind of interference and he would answer to Peregrine for his work, and a certain small sum of money by way of remuneration.

He had during his wanderings met many such name-less people who rejoiced in their own sense of power, in however small a sphere: narrow, set and unyielding to any human frailty of feeling.

'Well, let's get on now.'

They left the office and turned into the main room behind the screens. It was a large room. Down the centre were ranged, practically touching each other, white iron beds, with only a small enough space between each to house a little table, and room for the occupant to remove himself.

Titus could see that some of the beds were occupied, while others had been made and were empty. At the end of the room, in a large alcove, were chairs of every description, some with restraining bars, which formed a circle at the wall's edge. Most of the chairs were occupied by dormant human beings. The lack of animation was the most noticeable aspect. Not even the eyes showed any sign of life. Each man was an island. Each island was too remote to link with any other. Mist, fog, a moonless night separated island from island, and the vegetation, which at one time might have been receptive to cultivation, was barren; no future could be seen, even if it had been possible to coax the tiniest particle of life into being.

But among these sad remnants, who were still, there were some who could not stop moving. One stood in a corner of the room, jumping up and down with the tirelessness of a child and with as little purpose. Another, obsessed by perpetual motion, walked at great speed round and round the ward and, if the french windows on to the garden were open, made his lolloping way anticlockwise, passing little groups moving with the help of male nurses at the pace of a tortoise.

Titus noticed one man, who shiftily walked up the ward and drank from the bottles beside any occupied bed.

Peregrine showed him what his tasks would be. Titus had never had very much to do with children, and his own childhood, which had been unlike any other, gave him very little clue as to how a child's mind worked. He imagined that these men he now saw had entered the second stage of juvenilia, but the resemblance ended there, as he was to learn later.

The duties Titus was to undertake were menial. The washing and shaving of those whose limbs or faculties were beyond such a daily exercise. Dressing and undressing those who could not or would not help themselves. Feeding others who had no fancy to eat, or if they had, were not capable of doing so, so that their clothes gave off a sickly odour from the food that had been dropped. In two or three of the beds, Titus was told, were men, old soldiers who had been in them for nearly fifty years, their young manhood smothered for ever by a gas that had taken the whole sweetness of life from them, in a war forgotten by nearly everyone. Another man, upright like a soldier, stood all day issuing commands to a ghost platoon. Unlike the others, he was clean and almost as young looking as on the day that whatever had happened to stultify his hopes and expectations had happened. Only he, among these lonely men, seemed happy and carefree in his own isolated world.

The days went by with a lack of hope and very little laughter, but Titus found friendship with the other men who worked with him. There seemed to be no world outside, and he confined himself to what he had to do. To think of what he was doing was at this time mentally beyond him, for strong as he was, by the end of each day he was physically exhausted. But later in his life he was to ask himself the reasons, to try to discover if there was anyone to blame for such meaningless destruction of so many human beings. He was nauseated by a great deal of what he had to do; to see the loss of dignity in men who at one time had been both loved and desired.

One day a man was brought to the ward on a stretcher and put to bed. He had been drugged to quieten him. His wife had come with him, and Titus watched as she brought out from a suitcase some books and pencils, some food and a few clothes, which she put in the small cupboard by the side of the bed.

There was something in the man that drew Titus to him, although he was in a deep, drugged sleep, and as she left to go the wife turned to him and said, 'Look after him, please. I will be down in two days' time.'

29

Intimations of Other Days

The daily duties could never cease. If some catastrophe had razed this building to the ground, with all its inmates in it, would it have mattered? But was it any more pointless than most of man's pursuits? The line between sanity and the loss of sentience became daily too perplexing for Titus to reach any conclusion, yet each day he helped to keep alive beings who hardly knew they were alive; and others who, knowing, did not wish it. Nevertheless, apart from one or two of the really unlovable among them, he was drawn to them by an indefinable feeling. A feeling that he had thought had died in him many years ago: compassion and protectiveness towards people from whom he neither wished nor expected to receive gratitude, and he knew that if there were ever any situation where there was a choice of leaving them to their fate, or saving their living bodies, he would save them, but no rational thought could explain this reasoning.

He had been told that the man who had been brought in some days before was an artist, and no one knew what was the matter with him. Titus remembered the pleading way in which the man's wife had asked him to look after her husband. When the effect of the drugs had worn off and with difficulty he sat up in his bed, one of the most pitiful sounds that Titus had ever heard almost rent the ward in two. A cry of despair. It belonged to neither man nor beast. It had in it all the pain that man has suffered since time began. It was so basic that it affected everyone, both staff and inmates, with an unnamed fear – such as the animal world feels before a natural disaster. The cries could not be alleviated by soothing words, or gentle persuasion. It was the soul and the heart of all humanity, pleading to whatever God there was for release.

The only release that was possible was an injection to quieten and deaden his consciousness and, being too frail to ward off the needle, he crumpled back on to the bed and slept, a heavy disturbed sleep.

The whole ward was in a turmoil, and it took Peregrine and Titus and two or three other men to calm it as best they could.

After the lunches were over, what few visitors ever came were allowed in.

At two o'clock the bell rang in the locked ward and

the door was opened. The artist's wife walked towards her husband's bed. He was still in his uneasy sleep. There was so little room that there was nowhere to sit except perched at the end of the bed. She put some things she had brought on the table and sat, looking at her husband with a look of longing, a palpable aching.

'How is he?' she asked, knowing that no one could say anything that could assuage so deep an affliction. Why or how should they, when surrounded by such an abundance of human disarray?

There was nothing for her to do but await his uneasy reawakening. The bell rang again, and an elderly woman walked the length of the bed-scape to the bed next to her husband, where an old man, sunken in cheek and jaw, lay dying. Another wife, another life. Each person, alienated in his own prison. This elderly visitor had taken on the unseeing eyes of those around her. She had no hope for the future, only a past that no one could share with her, her own husband included. She was not new to this world, as she sat upon a small stool by the bed. From time to time an emaciated hand struggled from the bedclothes and reached for an answering hand, and the smallest whisper emerged, and as the old woman touched his fingers, the artist's wife could just hear an echo from a world of years and years ago. 'Hold my hand, mother . . . mother . . . hold my hand,' then a rattle so faint as almost not to be heard, as the life in the bed floated away unobserved.

The only difference it made in the huge room was the arrival of a screen that now separated the quick (if that were not an exaggeration) from the dead.

The sleeping man in the next bed did not awake. The trumpets were too faint, and the two hours that had passed were over, and his wife had to leave.

Titus watched her as her steps took her back to the locked door and into the world outside. He did not take part in the formalities that followed the ending of a life, but once more, with his work companions, had to soothe the agitation of the living.

And so the days wore on, the nights wore out, the lives wore down. Titus was drawn daily to a feeling towards the artist that he could not explain to himself. As though there was an indefinable link between his life and that haunted man for whom he had to perform duties that in his younger days would have affronted his dignity. Despite the haggard eyes, the remnants of teeth discoloured and decaying from too many drugs, there was an intelligence so forceful that it probed the inner life of everyone in the ward. His words would not make the sentences that he searched for, and in his frustration he would hit out at those around him, but with so little force there was no danger for anyone. Titus watched sometimes as his wife handed him paper and pencil with which to draw, and as the hand faltered over a few marks, he would brush them away with a sigh so piteous and profound it almost rent his being.

Sometimes, when the day was fine, they would go out to the vast gardens, lovely and cared for. Huge, rich, generous rhododendrons of many degrees of red led to an apple orchard of old trees.

The artist could not walk without assistance, but dragged his feet and made no movement with his arms. Whichever arm was not in his wife's lay rigid, totem-poled to his side. Their progress was slow, but aware. The squirrels that teased their steps, and so endearingly cradled in their tiny human paws the crumbs and nuts that had been scattered to them, were a delight to them both. They would stand still, just looking, until the husband swayed on his feet; then an arm would act as a brake to forestall the inevitable fall backwards.

Sometimes, when the wife did not come and the weather was fine, Titus would clean and feed and dress the artist and take him out into the gardens himself, linking his arm for protection only. There was no verbal communication, for it had ceased. Only the eyes looked and searched Titus. The eyes saw. They, the only remaining conscious sense, were more alive than any eyes Titus had ever seen, in his childhood, adolescence, young manhood, in and out of every world that he had ever traversed. He felt understood. He was one with this man. Whatever physical humiliations he had to perform were nothing. The truth spoke from the eyes, as he had never before heard, but sometimes when the tragedy seemed too intense the eyes smiled and a little gesture like a clown's would be conjured up by the deprived hands, and Titus could smile back, and for a few moments there was peace.

Towards the artist's wife also Titus felt the same closeness. Never very articulate, he had no need here, either, of verbal communication. They all seemed to be one person. He automatically performed all his duties outside these two. He was efficient, kind and far from lazy, and was respected by his companions, who all the same noted with surprise his affection for the patient in bed 10.

There was not always much said between the men who carried out their duties in the ward and the pompous officials who by their demeanour showed their importance, but it was with a great sense of shock that Titus was told one morning to get the artist ready to leave. Not that he was cured, but that he should never have been sent there in the first place. He had an illness that did not belong with them, and he was being sent elsewhere. His wife would go with him in an ambulance and that would be that. Titus must see that he was shaved, dressed as cleanly as possible and fed, and oversee his removal from the ward to the car.

The morning dawned and the wife arrived. Titus fulfilled many duties, then turned to bed 10. He shaved, dressed and cleaned the poor limbs, and made the patient ready for the departure. The man had all the intuition of an animal, which knew that something was about to happen that would affect his life, and a terrible restlessness manifested itself. He tried to move, and the wife sat in a chair by him, trying to calm him, showing him books, which she told Titus were his work. He pushed them aside with an impatience of gesture that for all the sluggishness of movement was a powerful negation of ownership.

The day wore on, and there was no sign of departure. It was not until late afternoon that a chair, with none of the elegance or grandeur of a sedan chair, was brought by two men into the ward, and the patient from number 10 bed was lifted into it and wrapped like a mummy in red blankets. The little procession made its way out of the ward, gathering the few paltry possessions, and Titus took the wife's arm and followed with her, down the long, bleak, dimly lit corridors, and out into the grey evening to the waiting ambulance. As the patient was lifted into the back of it he made a final gesture of farewell, and a faint voice whispered, 'Titus.'

30

Happening in a Side Street

Not for the first time in his life Titus felt the void that parting opens up so violently, but in this case it was not he who had left. He could feel a little of the sense of loss he had inflicted on so many people. An emptiness when he awoke, and when he went to bed, and all during the day when he was working. An ache he had only once before felt. He had lost something irreplaceable, but no rational explanation came to him as to why he should have such strong feelings for a man who had not spoken, whose outer life was destroyed, but whose eyes and inner life haunted him.

He knew that he wanted to leave the hospital and let his life drift wherever it took him. He spoke to Peregrine, who only expressed surprise that he had stayed at all. There were no formalities and nothing to await, no farewells, no broken hearts. He left, walking down the long drive, and as he reached the lodge and the large iron gates, which shut in or out this world within a world, the heavy sense of his own secret and unexplained loss became intolerable, and he let his legs lead him, for neither his head nor his heart could do so.

As he walked along the isolated road, he could just see the tower on the hill to his right, which brooded over the enclosed world he had left. As far as he could see, in every other direction was scrubland. Barren and bleak and unbeloved. Gorse bushes and bracken. He was in tune with this landscape as he walked. He saw no human beings and very little in the way of traffic. He was passed once by an old woman riding an antiquated tricycle. In the front of it was a basket from which appeared the heads of a motley collection of dogs, their bodies covered by an old blanket.

His feet led him along the road, and he felt neither tired nor active. He refused to think of anything. Ahead of him he began to see the lights of a town. He had money in his pocket with which to find some place to stay, and he continued walking. It must have been a couple of hours, and the light began to go as he neared the outskirts. A few scattered dwellings to begin with, then the dreary uniform dinginess of terraced houses.

As the daylight faded, so he saw ahead of him the rectangles of yellow-lit windows, and the skyline of the town taking on its untidy silhouette, with here and there the ugly uncompromising blocks, which seemed to bear no relation to the rest of the townscape. Coming closer to human beings, he started to feel an intense hunger, and despite his mental lethargy, he began to increase his speed of walking.

As on the outskirts of most towns and cities, there seemed little life, on or out of the street. The lights from the windows were gradually extinguished by the drawing of curtains. Towards the end of a line of houses he noticed that one of them had its curtains drawn to display two large candles in the window, and there was a certain amount of activity; people in ones and twos and threes making their way to its front door, which was ajar, and disappearing behind it. Titus heard the murmur of voices and muted footsteps overtaking him. A man and a woman drew level with him, 'Good evening. A sad evening this – yes, yes. She was a fine woman. A fine woman.'

Titus found himself on the inside of the pavement and had no choice but to turn towards the partly open front door as the two strangers turned inevitably in the same direction. The man was small and aggressive and the woman, a head taller, held his arm, seemingly more to protect him from his own aggressiveness than herself against the butts of others. Titus now saw that she held a wreath in her other hand, as they pushed open the door and entered the house.

There was a strong smell of incense and a low

murmur, the drone of people at prayer. The hall was narrow and dark, and to the left was a closed door, but passing this, Titus was slowly propelled to a second door at the farther end of the narrow passage. All three entered the room, which retained an atmosphere of a bygone age. It was cluttered with the past. The walls and the tables and the chairs were sepia. There were gas jets and a flounce over the fireplace.

As the incongruous companions were shown to some upright chairs, an elderly lady took their hands in turn. She was dressed in unrelieved black. Her severe hair was black, and drawn tightly behind her ears into a bun at the nape of her neck. Jet earrings and a high jet collar must have all but choked her. Her eyes were like two beads from the collar, and the only thing which was not black were the red rims of her eyes.

'You would like to see her, of course, before you take tea.'

People were sitting in rows of chairs facing a sliding door, which separated the back room from the front, and as it slid slowly open, those in the front row moved forward, and everyone else moved, as in some game for children, so that there was an all change, but done with no laughter, and no sound apart from a sigh and a sob and a sniff of stifled tears from one or other of the women present.

As some departed, others came in to take their places, and soon Titus found himself in the front row. He was the only person with no offering, but the absorption of sorrow precluded any kind of censure. He had at least come to pay his respects.

It was now his turn to go behind the door, into the front room. He had no wish to encounter death again. He entered the room he had seen from the outside, lit by two candles. Incense, and the flowers that were laid in banks all around the room, nearly felled Titus by their power, and his hunger pangs turned to nausea and a longing to run away from the raised open coffin he was to look into.

The tall lady gave a sob, as she leaned over and touched the cheek of the mourned. Titus closed his eyes as he passed, but with the native curiosity of human beings he was unable to prevent himself from opening them as he himself came near.

He looked, and was filled once more with the unexplained mystery of death. Although he neither knew nor cared about the being that was laid out so carefully in its solid coffin, what lay there surely bore little relation to what it had been. He remembered the deaths of people he had known and loved, known and hated, known and cared little about. But in them all was the common denominator. The enigma. Where were they? They did not all look peaceful. In some it seemed their torments were not all over. They did not look like real people, but they did not look like wax people either. They were not there, in that body left behind, to be disposed of in such a variety of ways, yet the idea of any kind of physical desecration or insult was unthinkable, like deliberately pulling the wings off a butterfly, or destroying a flower for the sake of it. The dead must be handled with care.

So, in this ordinary little house, the death of one of its former inmates had bestowed on everyone living the magic wand of mystery. As Titus left the room of the dead, he was shown out of the door and pointed to a room at the end of the narrow passage. On a table in the middle were plates of sandwiches and numerous cups. This whole room gleamed with cleanliness, and another lady with black hair and eyes and earrings and dress poured tea into the small delicate cups from a very large silver teapot.

No one spoke as they stood around the table, passing plates to each other. An occasional murmur of 'a wonderful woman. We shall not see her like again' brought hankies out to gather up the tears such words inevitably cause to flow.

Titus ate and longed to escape from this strange little interlude. As he turned to leave, the elderly second dark lady turned to him and quietly thanked him for coming.

An old overfed dog looked at him, with eyes that seemed to gut him. He moved along the passage and to the front door. Two old ladies, and an old man, were on their way out. They turned to Titus as they stood on the pavement and said, 'You must be the great-nephew. How sad you came too late. She was a fine woman.'

As they turned and walked away, the old man on the arm of each old lady, Titus had a strong feeling that he would for ever be an onlooker in life and death.

31

Under the Masks

Titus might have been numbered amongst the dispos-sessed by a bureaucratic mind, but this would have greatly underestimated him. He was dispossessed by his own act of will. He possessed nothing except himself. He took no care, but did he ever long for an anchorage? Was there no harbour that he craved? Did he not some-times think with longing for the cover of a retreat from the anarchic shapelessness of his life? If not material possessions then did he yearn for one love, so that he could belong somewhere? So that he could have a label? So that he could be identified as so-and-so, who was such-and-such, who came from here, and was going there?

If he had been asked such questions, he would have skidded around them. If he answered them to himself, he would probably have found no answer, as to *why* he wanted none of those things. But *what* he wanted in their stead was even more mysterious. He gathered experience, as a child might pick daisies, yet his daisy-chain was destined for no one's necklace or crown, but did the discarded little flowers wither within him as fresher daisies were picked? No, as time went by, his chain grew, and at appropriate moments he garlanded his chance encounters, and then, leaving them behind him, he could not stop himself from moving on.

People would say to him, 'You could write a book,' and he would answer, 'Yes, I could.'

Women whom he met wished to pin him down. He was elusive to them. A gentle imaginative lover who, when they thought he would share their life and love – if not for ever then for a mutually convenient length of time – would disappear as suddenly as he had arrived in their lives.

No one could exactly describe him. Either physically or mentally. He was not handsome in any accepted way. In company he was withdrawn, and yet he was not in the least shy. He had a certain sardonic wit, a quick response to the quirks of human beings. He laughed readily. He liked women. He was quiet. He was courteous, but upon discussion between themselves, those who knew him well would all reach the conclusion that despite all these things, *he* was not there.

He looked strong. In the years of wandering he had supported himself in every kind of physical pursuit which could be imagined, and lived and shared his being mainly with the rough, and the tough, whilst retaining his own persona. He was generous to the needy. He ate and drank robustly. He slept well. There was a normality about him which was a source of wonder to acquaintances. But still, they only saw the shell. What lay inside in heart or head, they never discovered. In whatever company he found himself, he adapted to it, but he was no chameleon, and he remained an outsider. He had seen cruelty, injustice and bigotry. He was not a reformer or a zealot, but whenever he came across these vices, he fought against them.

He decided to leave the black, dreary town, and make his way seawards. He had a longing to move away. He wanted to be a part of a wild landscape. Perhaps an island. Small but self-contained. To be surrounded, constricted, unable to wander further than each last rock. In his mind he heard the gulls, and it was with a shock that he became aware that he was no longer alone.

'Look, we've been following you, friend. You look as though we could use you, friend. You come quietly with us, and we'll tell you who we are. Come noisily, and you won't tell anyone anything again. See?'

'Well, it's rather dark.'

'Look, friend. We don't like jokes.'

Titus felt two people on either side of him, and a few

more behind. He had no choice but to walk in the direction in which he was being propelled.

The dingy street was left behind as the incipiently violent group made its way, in the growing dark, to what looked like a lodging house of a large estate. They entered through the front door, and it was obvious that the whole place was derelict, both from the smell of rot and the lack of any kind of human warmth or comfort. They pushed at Titus to follow them.

'We're going down, friend. We've got candles down there. You interested?'

'I'm interested.'

'Look friend, I told you we don't like jokes.'

The spokesman was small and his voice had a nasal pitch, as though he was holding his nose. They tripped their way down a small steep flight of stairs, and were enveloped in complete darkness, until the voice of command said, 'All right friends – light up.'

Matches were struck, and candles which were ready on boxes and in alcoves were lit. There were about six people illuminated by the candles, but all had their back to Titus, who stood in the middle of a cold earth-floored cellar. They were fumbling with their hands to their faces, until the voice of command ordered them to turn.

Each face wore a mask, made of what Titus took to be carnivorous animals and birds of prey.

'We're the "Destructionists", friend. There's only one word we like. Destroy. Destroy. Oh, yes. We like another one too. Hate. That's a good one. Got any ideas?'

'What about "Revolution"?'

'Look, friend, I told you no jokes.'

'I don't think that's funny.'

'Red, you can deal with him if he goes on being funny. Black, get out the papers. Vulture, go through his things. We don't believe in possessions, friend. Give anything he's got to Magpie, and then we'll get down to business.'

Vulture frisked him roughly. His mask was pathetically and crudely made. Whatever else this group of people had, they possessed no talent for transforming their ideas into artistic shape.

'Mangod, there's nothing. He hasn't got anything, except this bit of change.'

'Of course he has, haven't you friend? Everyone has, who looks like him. He's not one of us, are you, friend? Come on, where've you hidden them?'

'Hidden what?'

'Your things. Everyone has things. That's what we're for. Destroy. Take away. Replace nothing. Until there is nothing. *We* will control, because we will rule by hate. If you've not got things on you, you've got them some-where. Everyone has. You probably have a woman who says she "loves" you. They're good to get at. They can hate as quickly as they "love". We've got recruits everywhere. Come on, tell me where your things are. Pictures – they're good. Cut them up. Books – they're good. Burn them. Houses, flowers, animals, easy to destroy in any way that takes our fancy. Come on friend, out with it!'

'Strange to say, I have no "things" as you call them . . . friend.'

'No jokes, I said,' and the voice of command rose two octaves in its querulous frustration. And don't call me friend. I don't like your tone. I've had my eye on you. There's something about you I don't like, and I'll tell you what it is. You don't fit in but there's still something we can destroy. Good material. What's your name? Where do you live? Where are all your things? What do you believe and why? Now straight answers. No cheek from you, friend.'

'My name is Titus Groan. I come from a place you would never have heard of. I had great possessions. I left them. I live nowhere. I have nothing, except what you can see. I am on my way from one place to another, doing what work I can get, and I believe that each individual is more important than any social body. I am dependent on myself alone is about the longest sentence I have spoken for a long time . . . friend.'

'If you say friend again, I'll get Red to deal with you. *I* say friend, *not* you. Who do you hate?'

'I don't. Some years ago it may have been different. If I speak of *now* I am not involved enough or care enough, and destruction for its own sake is the fantasy of a failure. Why do *you* want to force your doctrines on others?'

'Look, friend, *I* ask the questions, and if I don't get better answers you'd better take care of what you say is all you possess – if that's all you've got, then I'll take that.'

'Are you afraid?'

'Red, at the ready . . .'

Red, hiding behind a mask so badly made that it was difficult to see what animal it was meant to represent, came up to Titus and pointed a knife at his throat.

Titus was sure adolescents lurked behind the masks. He didn't fear this hate-filled group whose only antidote to the emptiness of their lives was to seek to reduce the lives of others to their own level. He could see the cause of their ugly behaviour but he couldn't remedy it.

'Your name, it doesn't make sense. What does it mean, eh, friend? *And* don't be clever either.'

'If I told you, you wouldn't believe me, although you and your friends live in a fantasy. I'd rather keep my name to myself. You know you've got the wrong man in me. You don't frighten me. You threaten my life, which you are bound to accept is my only possession. If you take that, it'll only be a transfer – I'll become your possession then, but I can't quite think what use I'll be to you. A dead weight, that's dead sure . . .'

'You lot, I want Groan to myself and then I'll issue my orders. Get out, and quick. Face towards the wall, Groan.'

Titus leaned face against the wall, and listened to the clumsy footsteps making their way up the dark staircase.

'Alright. If you want to get away with your life, you'd better convince me, and good. Make me believe you. Talk!'

'Well, Mr Mangod. There is a great deal to say, and the night is far from young. Have you the stamina to listen for many hours to a tale such as you have never heard before? Why don't you remove your mask. Whichever way I leave here, dead or alive, I'll not give away your secret. I've spent enough time running, from more things than you have ever encountered . . .'

'Who says so?'

'Well, no one, but Mr Mangod, forgive me if I hazard a guess that the years on your back do not add up to as many fingers and toes you carry?'

Defeated, Mangod pulled the mask from his face.

A boy of around seventeen stood before Titus. He had tow-coloured hair, cropped short, and dark eyes set close together, a high forehead gave the impression of an intelligence deeper than he possessed. His body was thin and undernourished. Titus felt a surge of pity for him. He sympathised with this youth whose yearning for something other than his own life led him into following this path that didn't promise even a whisper of success.

'Groan, I knew you weren't right when you started to talk – or even before. That's why I've sent the others away. I can't lose face in front of them. You've got some-thing I want.'

'What's that?'

'I can't pin it down. Other people would have been afraid. I don't know if you're brave, or if you don't care. I'll never be like you. I've got to be top, even if it's only in a miserable little hole like this. But you haven't laughed at me. Why not, eh, Groan?'

Titus didn't say that there was so much more to pity than to laugh at.

'I don't want to hear your story. I just want you to go now. I'll have to live this down with them, you know, and someone's going to pay for it. Get out now, Groan, and keep out of my way.'

Titus shuffled up the dark stairs, out into the fresh air.

32

A Sanctuary

Once more he walked, and after some time he found himself out of the run-down end of the town, and from the feel and silence of his new environment he imagined himself to be on the edge of a wood, or common land. There were no lights to guide him, but his feet no longer felt concrete beneath them. A grass verge he felt by touching it with his shoe, as a blind man traces the shape of objects by the touch of his fingers, and as he walked further, so that verge became larger and softer, and he found himself preferring to walk on the grass. He became aware of a high shape to his right, and it drew him to it like a magnet. As he reached it, this time his hands explored, and they diagnosed a wall, quite a rough wall, but high and impenetrable. He thought of it as something he could rest against, not of something that was keeping him out. His fatigue guided him and he sank down, obliterating thought and hunger, and slept, with no dreams, but a thankfulness for the overpowering oblivion he was vouchsafed.

'Good morning, my son.'

Titus heard these words, but he didn't know if he heard them or if he dreamed them.

'Good morning, my son,' he heard again, and again. Then he opened his eyes, and closed them, to hear the words once more. He sat up. It was light now. His hand touched a wall and damp grass, and with difficulty he sat up. An old man, with a fringe of white hair, dressed in a black robe, was before him.

'Ah, you're awake now. And what, may I ask, and how and why, may I ask, brings you to us?'

'Oh, I think there are too many answers, too many questions.'

'Well, my son, if you are hungry come with me, and there shall be no more answers to no more questions. May I suggest you come with me?'

Titus stood up with difficulty. His back was twisted, or so it felt, as he tried to reach his height. He thought that some unseen hand had hit him a sideways blow in the small of his back as he tried to straighten up, or that blunt knives were being stuck in it at irregular intervals.

An old dog, that had been sniffing the wall, came slowly up to him and looked at him with that frightening trust dogs possess.

Titus shook off the sensation of knives and became himself. 'Yes, I *am* hungry. I have no idea where I am, though.'

'Well, why not come with me, then? I was just walking. Although old Trouper has space and plenty, he likes to explore the outer walls. He and I are given dispensation. We're both old now, and age confers one or two blessings. Come, young man.'

In the oncoming daylight, the three made their slow way along the edge of the wall until they came to some large stone pillars with, between them, a wooden door of enormous dimensions. To one side of it was a smaller door, which was ajar, and through this they went.

They were walking up an overgrown path to a drawbridge, over an overgrown moat, and Titus saw ahead of him a large building. There were ecclesiastical-looking windows. They walked towards what must have been the front door. Two men in black robes were raking pink gravel into patterns like waves and, as the trio passed and displaced some of the waves, they raised their heads and nodded a silent welcome.

They passed into the hall and a feeling of sanctuary overcame Titus. There was no sound. There was an order and a cleanliness that he had not witnessed for a long time, if ever. It had nothing to do with the polish he had been aware of in the houses of the rich or the house-proud, but it seemed to have a purpose. He became aware of his own ramshackle appearance.

'I'll show you, first of all, to your room. You might like to cleanse yourself, after your night out, my son, and then there'll be breakfast with the other guests. You couldn't have chosen a better time for me to find you.'

They walked down a corridor with doors spaced evenly all the way, until they came to one, which the old man opened. 'This one is free.'

It was a small, whitewashed room, with a small iron bed, and a stand with a water jug and basin. It looked out upon a lawn with a cedar tree, and the lawn sloped down to a stream.

'I'll come back in ten minutes and take you to the refectory, and you can meet your fellow guests. Then I'll take you to meet the Prior. We don't ask questions, you know. If you have some money to spare we should be pleased, but if you haven't then you can do a little work. There is always plenty to do.'

When the door had closed, Titus looked out of the window and saw a squirrel, standing upright, with its hands cradling something it had found on the grass, before turning and speeding away with it to its secret hideaway.

The water in the jug was cold, but as he poured it into the basin and covered his face, his whole spirit lightened and the pervading serenity of the house was almost tangible.

A knock came on the door. The old man had said he would return.

'Well, then, my son. Do you feel fresher now and ready for your breakfast? Come, follow me.'

They walked back down the corridor and through the hall, until they reached a large oak door, through which could be heard the sound of cutlery and china being used. The old man opened the door and motioned to Titus to follow. The room they entered was low and spacious: oak-panelled, and lit by three windows the height of the room, which looked on to a garden that was cared for just as everything was that he had seen.

A long refectory table took up practically the length of the room and, as the old man led him to it, Titus saw that people were sitting on both sides of it. They were silent as they ate but sitting on a slightly raised dais at the far end of the room was a man reading aloud. Titus sat on the seat to which he had been shown and, though no one was speaking, his needs were attended to with deft and silent speed.

Everything that was passed to him had the goodness of food made by hands that wanted to make it. The goodness of the food overwhelmed Titus and he was so hungry that he was hardly aware that he was not alone, and it was not until he could eat no more that he raised his eyes and looked across the table.

He had been aware of an agitation, which seemed alien in the peace of the room, and he froze on his chair as he met the eyes of the man opposite. The eyes that looked deeper and beyond any eyes he had ever seen, except once before. They were the same eyes. It was the same man.

As he looked at the other guests at the table, he could see that they were mostly men, and for whatever reason they had found their way to this retreat, they had, all but one, succeeded in achieving the inner and the outer peace they had come for. Only a dreadful restlessness, both of body and spirit, seemed to consume the man with whom he felt an affinity that was inexplicable.

A chair jerked backwards, tearing into the polished floor, and the dreadful screech obliterated the quiet voice of the reader. He had left the room, with a slow shuffle, and when he had closed the door Titus made up his mind to seek him out.

The meal ended in the refectory, and as it ended each person stood for a moment while a prayer of thanks was said. The room emptied and outside small groups of people spoke together, quietly, but creating the impression that each was absorbed completely in his own universe.

One youngish man came up to Titus and in a friendly way suggested he might care to see the gardens and the buildings, but before he had time to answer the old man came up to him and said he would like to take him to the Prior.

They crossed the hall once more and went through a door marked PRIVATE. This divided what must have been the inner world from the outer. Though glistening, it was spartan and bare, and when the old man knocked a voice of extreme cultivation bade them come in.

'This is the young man who came with me.'

'Ah, yes. Welcome.'

'I have told him we don't ask questions.'

'That is true. But may I tell you that we have some rules. Silence in the refectory, you have already seen (if not heard!). We sleep early, and our guests do not stay late in bed. Each one is responsible for his own room. There is contemplation, but no one is asked to do anything. The people who come here all come for different reasons, but paramount for all of them is, I hope, the peace, the cleansing and the rejuvenation of their spirit, or call it what you will. You can help in any of the pursuits in the running of this house and garden, if you would care to, but if you do not wish it there is no obligation. I hope that while you are here you may find inner peace.'

'Perhaps I am here under false pretences, for I did not come. I was found.'

'Yes, I have been told, but once more I would like to say, we ask no questions. Peace go with you, my son.'

The interview was ended, and Titus and the old man left the Prior.

'I would like to ask you something,' said Titus to the old man.

The old man nodded his assent and Titus said, 'The man . . . the man in the refectory.'

'Ah, yes. We have a little knowledge, but it is not for me to break into his seclusion. I cannot.'

'I know him – I have seen him. I feel as though there is a link I cannot explain.'

'Perhaps that is what led you here. Who can say? I am very old and I have seen how strange are the mani-festations of whatever spirit you believe in. There is nothing that cannot happen. Yes, my son, I see in him a quest, a search, a reaching beyond what might be too great for one human being. He may be too far away for us, but I have watched him in the gardens, in the house, and the wealth within is breaking the locks, overflowing. There is tenderness. I have seen him fondling a bird with a broken wing, and mend it as best he could. I have seen him looking, looking, until he could look no more, at everything around. I have seen him play with the children who come here to lend a hand. He was at one with them and they with him. He has done drawings for them. I have seen him laughing with them, and making little jokes. I have never seen him hurt any living person or thing. And yet, my son, he causes discomfort. The guests do not understand, and I think he will have to leave. He is restless. So restless. He disturbs them. At night he cannot sleep. I have found him many times. His words will not come, and his sighs break my heart. I have led him back to his room and remade his bed as many as ten times in one night. Sometimes he falls, for his steps are halting, and his feet drag almost as though there were an invisible ball and chain on them. And when he wishes to thank me, and cannot, then is the only time I see anger in his eyes. There are paper and pencils and pens in his room, and drawings, and there is writing and the room is untidy. Sometimes, when his words come, he talks to the Prior, and with the intelligence there is so much humour. What can I say, my son? To understand such things is not for me to query. Can I accept? It is not for me. I am simple, and my life has been simple. I have no answers. I do accept. I do pray. But I am sure that he will have to leave. There are so many here who have come for rest and quiet, and we owe it to them to allow them that pleasure.'

'Thank you.'

Titus left the old man and walked back to his quarters. It had been some time since he had been alone, in a physical way, and his sense of well-being exacerbated his lassitude, and he slept heavily, waking only when the day was almost over. The silence everywhere gave him no clue of time, but he reached for a small light near his bed, and the light gave him the impetus to jump up, before he had time to think about doing so.

He made his way out into the corridor and, like an animal in search of food, he turned towards the refectory. The animal sense that had awakened him proved right, for it seemed that a meal had just begun.

He saw his fellow guests raise their eyes at his entrance, with varying degrees of welcome and recognition, and he took his place where he had breakfasted. The eyes of the man opposite watched as he sat down, and his hunger abated as he felt his stomach flip. He could see by the eyes and the faltering hands, which played with the food on the plate, that the restlessness that could not be concealed was becoming too big a burden, and the strident screech of the chair on the floor once more broke the silence, striking a note of discord. Although the fellow guests tried to hide their feelings, there were one or two who raised their eyebrows and shook their heads, as they watched the sad, stumbling exit of the man they did not seem to understand.

Titus could no longer stay. He followed, and it was not long before he overtook the man. He was standing. His eyes were closed and he seemed rooted to the floor. His legs were too heavy to move, but he could not stand upright without swaying. Titus put out his arm as a prop and held the swaying body. The man made to move one leg with the diffidence of a child learning to walk, and in his frailness he would have fallen, save for the protective arm.

'Thank you,' a voice with no strength behind it whispered.

The two figures stood in the silent corridor, waiting for the momentum that would once again start up the faulty engine.

They stood for some minutes as the legs and arms jerked as though they did not belong to the torso that owned them, then suddenly the engine restarted, and Titus was surprised by the speed with which they moved along the corridor to a room like his own, but alive with a life of its own, untidy mounds of paper on the table and crumpled balls of paper thrown around in disarray. Plus bottles of ink and paints. There were drawings, and sheets of paper with writing on them, and it seemed that they were the sustenance of life, that here were the warlocks, almost the vehicles of destruction of a man's life, but at the same time the very reason for his living.

The man made his way to the bed, as to a sanctuary, and with a cry, a rabbit in a snare, laid himself down upon it and closed his eyes.

There was nothing Titus could do, and by the time he had reached the door that dreadful restlessness grabbed its victim again, and before he was quite out of the room he saw the faltering figure slide off the bed, go to the table and, sitting at it, take up a pencil and make marks upon some paper.

33

An Unwelcome Interlude

Titus made his way to his own room. He had no wish for company. As the light woke him, he had an uneasy feeling that he had betrayed himself. He lay thinking and then he knew that he had wanted to be on hand when inevitably during the night that dreadful illness would take hold of the man to whom he was so inexorably drawn.

He went to the refectory, but found it empty. He was either too early, or too late. There seemed no one about. He made his way to the garden, and there he saw his old friend. He crossed the lawn to where he was raking up leaves into tidy piles and said, 'Good morning. I'm looking . . .'

'Yes, my son. It was as I feared. We had to phone his wife early this morning and he was put on a train, to be met. There was nothing else to be done. I stayed with him, and we walked the house together all during the night, but there have been so many complaints, what else was there to do? Left to myself, I would have taken charge of him, but I must take my orders, you know.'

'I understand, but for all your kindness and the serenity here, I couldn't stay. I don't understand what has happened to me. I must go. For the first time in all my wanderings I feel there *is* a purpose, and fate, or whatever controls my destiny may lead me there.'

'Perhaps I can understand a little more than you think – or perhaps *not* understand, but grasp a little. For all my simple way of life, my lack of what you might call "experience", I have seen all manner of men come here, and seek in so many ways to lay down their burdens.'

'I think you are *good*. I too have seen all manner of people. Eccentric, greedy, rich, poor, ambitious, beautiful, crippled, but very seldom . . . good. It is an untouchable quality. I don't think cynicism could ever hurt you, or destroy you.'

'Oh, my son. I have been out of temptation's way. Who knows what I might have become if I had not been sheltered here?'

'In my very brief stay here, you are the only one . . . but then, that man. It was a different quality. I saw truth there, for all the pain. Intangible. Yes, I must go now, and thank you for every kindness to him.'

'Before you go you must have some food. Come with me. We'll go to the kitchen.'

They walked together through the refectory, and into a large, airy kitchen that adjoined it. It was painted a brilliant azure and the stone floor was scrubbed nearly white. There was a huge wooden table, bleached to the colour of the palest wine. Everything in it glistened, as did everything in the whole house. In a basket by a vast kitchen range lay a tabby cat, licking endlessly one or other of her newly born little brood of blind offspring. There was no one else in the room, but freshly cut vegetables and fruit shone on the white table, and their green and red seemed to give point to the deep azure walls.

The old man opened cupboards, and brought out bread and honey and butter, and placed them in front of Titus. 'Now then, eat away, and I'll make you something to drink, and I'll give you a packet to be on your way.'

He finished the food that had been provided and, standing up, he said, 'I would like to leave some money for all that I have received, and perhaps you would say goodbye to the Prior for me.'

'I will say goodbye, but don't leave any money. If at some time you can spare a little it would be welcome, but not now. Goodbye, my son, and peace go with you.'

Titus left the way he had come, and found himself once more on the road. It was still early in the morning, and there were no people and no vehicles. He walked on the grass verge, by the side of the wall that had been a bedpost in his fatigue.

Before he had been waylaid he had made up his mind that he would make his way towards the sea. He had spent little of his life on the sea; although he had voyaged far and wide on many different craft, it was not native to him and he had a certain fear of it. Perhaps it was one of the few things he was afraid of.

A very large antiquated black car drew up beside him. It stopped, and from the back window that had been unwound he saw a head appear and a voice, which was neither obviously male or female, called out, 'Going our way?'

Titus was tired of chance encounters and he made no answer, expecting whoever it was to drive away, but the unwieldy vehicle backed slowly, until it drew up beside him.

'I said, going our way?' repeated the voice.

'Well, I'm not sure where I'm going.'

'In that case you're the boy for me. I know just where I'm going. Get in.'

'I really want to go on not knowing where I'm going, until I get there.'

'More and more elaborately amusing. A puzzle – an enigma. My very taste, but I *will* not take no.'

The door was opened and the occupant got out. He was a portly man, dressed in a formal black suit. His face was sharp, his mouth was small and rather mean, and his hair, what little of it there was, was brushed straight back from a low forehead.

'Now then, look in here. You simply can't refuse. Have you ever seen anything like it?'

Titus looked inside; the car seemed to contain every comfort on wheels that could be imagined. A table set with ornate and highly polished silver. Roses in a silver bowl, a bookshelf filled with leather-bound books; a white velvet seat and a rug on the floor with all the faded beauty of antiquity.

'I'm hardly dressed to compete, am I?'

'There *could* be no competition. *I* do not compete. What I possess is always the best. Come, get in, and you can listen to my poems. I was tiring of my own definitely stimulating company and there is still some way to go. Come, I insist.'

Titus had no wish to sit near this man, who for all his eccentricity did not appeal to him, but he had neither the strength nor the positive will to refuse. So he got in, cautious of the damage his shoes might do to the incredibly beautiful rug.

The man took an apparatus beside him and speaking into it in his unpleasant high-pitched voice said, 'Advance.'

The vehicle glided noiselessly and effortlessly off, as though no mechanism existed in its antiquated but superlative body.

By the side of the man were sheafs of papers, which he at once took into his hands and from which he started to read. He made no attempt to introduce himself.

Titus realised that he was an ear only, and he ceased to listen as the voice, pleased to have an audience, mercilessly pursued its way through page after page of salacious verbiage.

They glided through a countryside whose beauty was lessened by the self-indulgent pronouncements of the sybarite.

'Well. Tell me, sweet youth. Have you heard such verse?'

'I have heard nothing like it,' Titus said truthfully.

'Ah. A youth whose taste belies his physical condition.'

The recitation was finished and, leaning forward, the man pressed a button at his side, and a small cupboard opened to display heavy crystal glasses and decanters. Pouring a pale liquid into two glasses, he handed one to Titus. 'To my muse. I bask headily in her arms.'

Titus raised his glass, but had no wish to join in the toast. He had an overwhelming desire to be away from this man whose grubby spirit tainted everything he contacted. 'I would like to get out now,' he said.

'Sweet youth. Be silent. We approach the very portals, ere long, of divinity. I would not deprive you of your chance to bathe (metaphorically speaking of course) in the waters of supreme beauty.'

As the voice grated on to its own delight, the car turned to the right. There were no gates, but a sign on a small board, with an arrow stated 'To Hidden House'.

They drove along what was a mixture between a rough cart track and a driveway. On both sides was a coppice, which looked uncared for, so deep and tangled were the roots and the ivy growing up the dead trees with great parasitic profusion. The road had a slight incline, but despite its bad condition it had no effect on the silky progress of the car.

As it sailed upwards, Titus wondered where the house could be, since there was no sign of one ahead, but he had decided to remain silent to his unattractive companion. The road now became rather twisting and the trees on either side sparser. He saw what appeared to be the roof of a large house, with a conglomeration of chimneys, both tall and squat.

'We approach, dear boy.'

The car drew effortlessly to a halt and the driver, whom Titus had not seen and had given no thought to, got out from his driving seat and appeared at the car door, on its owner's side. He was very small, very young and very frail, and his cast of features was also small, with hooded eyes. He seemed far too delicate to be in charge of such a large vehicle.

He opened the door and his master got out. Titus followed and found himself looking down at a great house, which seemed to grow out of the ground far below. The car had stopped beside a small wooden gate, and as it was opened, he saw steps that had been forged out of the rock, spiralling downwards. He imagined whoever lived in this strangely located house would suffer from a fairly strong feeling of claustrophobia.

The nameless man started his descent of the rough-hewn steps and motioned to Titus to follow. Despite his portly figure he was nimble on his feet, and they went downwards quite speedily. As they neared the end of the steps the house came into view more clearly. It was large and it seemed to have no particular shape. There were three floors, with four deep windows on either side of the front door. It was painted white and there was a courtyard in front, which allowed a breathing space between the last of the steps and the house itself.

The door was open, and the entrance room was painted white, with white-painted floorboards. Titus had imagined it would be gloomy but the atmosphere was translucent. The hall itself went right through to the back of the house, and a great glass window gave on to a large expanse of lawn, which seemed to have been recently cut.

There was a sound of voices and the man turned towards a door, once more indicating that Titus should follow. He entered a long drawing room. Again, there was the shock of whiteness. The floor, walls, ceiling, curtains, furniture, broken only by riotous colour in huge vases of flowers dispersed around the room at different heights. A woman, dressed in white, with abundant dark hair pulled back severely, sat on a sofa, with a child on her knee. They were playing a game with coloured beads, and she made no effort to rise on seeing her visitors.

'We thought you were coming last night.'

'My muse would have none of it. Here is a youth who knows not where he is bound, nor will do so until he arrives. Such enigmas are my daily bread. I shall retire to refresh myself, and the reading will begin after dinner. Farewell.'

Titus was left alone with the woman and child. She was too old to be the child's mother, but had a proprietorial air towards her surroundings.

'Run along now,' she said to the child, who jumped off her lap and ran out of the room.

'You must excuse me,' said Titus. 'I am a most unwelcome guest, I am sure. I'll leave now . . .'

'Oh, is it as dreadful as all that here?'

'No, but I feel that perhaps I am?!'

'You know, or of course you don't, when he comes, we never know what to expect, or rather, should I say we know enough to know that we do not know what to expect. Do you understand? And if I may say so, I am sure that you are probably more confused than I am.'

'Well, perhaps my own way of life has adapted me to the surprises that seem to hover wherever I go.'

'Is that exciting?'

'It was. But I've grown tired of them. When your friend elected me to be a captive ear, I was on my way somewhere else.'

'He is not exactly a friend. If that sounds disloyal, perhaps it is. He is one of those people that nearly everyone has in his or her life. He comes in and out of it, like summer storms. Everything is passive; then he arrives and devastation follows. He goes nowhere without leaving a trail behind him. However unpleasant the trail, it is at least memorable, and despite the fact that you didn't want to come, perhaps you would like to stay the night, and I can promise you it won't be dull. May I show you a room to sleep in?'

As she asked this question, the woman stood up, and Titus saw that she was a good deal older than he had thought. She was very tall and had slim legs. There were dark rings under her eyes, but there was a quizzical intelligence in them.

They left the white room and, passing across the hall, went through a door on the other side to a wide uncarpeted staircase painted white. As they went up three flights of stairs, Titus heard children's voices, laughing and querulous and being exercised with all the lack of inhibitions known to children.

'I expect they're dressing up. We've got a little theatre in the garden, you know,' the woman said. 'I hope you won't mind this room. The others are all occupied. It *was* a nursery – and they still use it.'

She spoke, as many people do, as though everything that happened in her house was common knowledge.

'We'll have dinner about eight.'

'I have no change of clothes – only what I came in. Perhaps you would rather . . .'

'Oh, we are very informal here, you know.'

It was a household, certainly, where the hostess (or so Titus assumed her to be) took everything in her stride.

'With a family like mine, I have long since learned to be surprised at nothing. Well, do make yourself at home.' And with that she left Titus in a much lived-in room, full of discarded toys and books – and all the paraphernalia of childhood, and in one corner an iron bedstead with bedclothes that had obviously seen other guests.

Titus found himself angry at having been so easy a pawn in what he thought of as his last accidental encounter, and he decided to leave, realising that his departure would make as little difference, in this haphazard house, as his arrival.

He was travelling light, so he left the nursery and started on his way downstairs. But his departure was not to be so easily accomplished.

'Oh, hello,' he heard, as a door opened to reveal laughter and music and singing.

'Hello,' he said, peering at two young faces that bore a resemblance to the dark woman he thought of as the 'lady of the house'.

'I expect you've come for tonight. We've more or less finished everything now. Shall we go down to the lake?'

'Well, I was just about to go,' began Titus, but was interrupted by a young girl, who said, 'But you've only just come. You can't go when you've just arrived. We'd think you didn't like us.'

It was too difficult for Titus to explain his arrival, so he decided that for tonight he would drift into whatever lay in store and erase his own wishes until the morning.

He found himself in a group of people much younger than himself, and he felt so far away in time and experience from them that he could not join with their lighthearted chatter; yet they tried to draw him into their activities with an easy friendliness. He thought he must appear dour to them, but his mind reverted continually to the man who had left his life so empty on two occasions. He did not wish to banish the memory of those eyes from his thoughts.

'You are far away,' said the same young girl to him. They were sitting by a lake, and Titus did not believe that this open garden could belong to the Hidden House. The back was entirely different from the front, but that seemed almost logical, with this likeable family.

'Would you like to see our theatre?'

'Yes, that would be nice.'

They walked across to the outbuildings, and the girl opened one of the stable doors and switched on a light. Inside was a stage at one end, and rows of assorted chairs. The walls were white-painted brick, and just beneath the raised stage was a decorated piano.

'I think we'd better go in. Some of the people may be coming soon. Did you come with "I am"?'

'If that's who I think it is, yes, I did.'

'Poor you. I expect you had the ordeal?'

'If that's what I think it is, yes, I did.'

'We've got it again tonight, you know. I wonder if anything will happen? It usually does. We'd better go now.'

They returned towards the back of the house, across

the lawn, and into the white drawing room through one of the long windows that looked on to the garden. There were people of all ages, in every kind of dress. There was nothing new in what Titus saw. He was loath to enter and, although his physical presence did so, his thoughts did not follow him. There was no need of speech – he merely appeared to listen to anyone who chose to speak *at* rather than *to* him. After an hour or so he realised that there was a common move from the white room towards a room across the hall.

34

The End of an Unwelcome Interlude

The large dining room with its white-clothed table running the whole length was ready: like a field awaiting the advance of the enemy.

About thirty people sat down at their allotted places, and the dark woman sat at one end of the table, with the chair at the other end remaining empty. The meal began, easy and friendly, and progressed quite happily for some time, until everyone became aware of a voice being raised outside the door. Titus recognised it, and he saw an interchange of raised eyes between his hostess and many of her guests.

The door was pushed open with a foot and in came the portly poet. His face was flushed and, as he sat down on the empty seat at the end of the table, he pointed a finger at a young man sitting a few places from him and spluttered, 'Be gone from this table. *You* do not sit with the great, and you, and you!' he screamed, pointing at other guests.

The meal had come to a standstill, and the reactions varied greatly. Some flushed, some grinned; only one vast woman of autocratic bearing continued as though there had been no interruption, which angered the bully more. He rose from his chair and, taking his glass of wine, before he could be stopped, poured it over her head. She continued eating, and the hostess, neither embarrassed nor angry, went up to him and led him away. She returned some minutes later and, taking her seat, spoke as though nothing had happened.

It took some time for most of the people to relax but gradually, as the room became warmer and the wine glasses more quickly refilled, a certain gaiety super-imposed itself and the mood regained its earlier ease.

Just as they were finishing the voice could be heard calling out, 'There will be murder in this house tonight.'

'I think you'd better get over to the theatre,' murmured the hostess to the girl, who must have been her daughter. 'Take the younger ones, and we'll come if we can. It looks an ominous evening ahead.'

The company divided into two camps – the younger ones leaving by a side door, and the older ones crossing the hall back to the white room.

'I am' was the only person there, and he was sitting in a big chair, beside him a table covered with what Titus recognised as the instrument of torture, which had nearly reduced him to crying for mercy that morning in the car. He knew that he could not endure another reading, and was on his way out when he was espied and called to.

'Come turn the pages, o slave.'

'I was about to leave. I must go.'

A deep flush rose on 'I am's' face, and his hostess whispered to Titus, 'Just once, to quieten him and then you will be free of him. Would you . . . please?'

How could Titus refuse? He was directed to a chair immediately behind the horrible man, who started to read. He read much of what he had done that morning, and as he finished each page, he threw it over his shoulder and extended his right hand for Titus to refill it with another paper. What he read was obscene and unoriginal, and each listening face betrayed an emotion of disgust or boredom or dislike. The more extreme the emotion shown, the more pleased the reader seemed, as he surveyed them, on reaching the end of each sheet of paper.

Suddenly a youngish man stood up and shouted, 'I've had enough,' and ran quickly out of the room.

The reading stopped and the poet, whose temper seemed hard to control, threw all his papers in the air and screamed, 'I'm not staying here. There will be murder in this house tonight. There will be murder. I shall walk to my house by the sea. There will be murder!'

So saying he departed, with all his papers scattered across the floors and chairs and, judging by the apoplectic sound of a door being slammed, left the house.

Someone picked up the papers, handling them with the disgust one might feel for a decomposing rat, and dropped them behind a chair, out of sight. The windows were opened and someone started to sing. Someone else told a joke, and there was the kind of laughter that people cannot control, after having been silent too long.

'What would you like to do?' asked the hostess.

'Nothing – just breathe fresh air,' said one person.

'Automatic writing,' said another.

'Oh, yes,' said a third, who pulled a round table to the middle of the room.

Chairs were placed round it, and those who wished sat down and put their hands, palms down, upon it.

Titus, longing to get out and away, watched in a desultory way. The lights had been lowered and there was a kind of hectic silence. Someone started to write, and as the table began to rise slowly from the ground, outside in the hall there was a sound of a horse's hooves. One of the women at the table gave a startled cry and the door of the room opened very, very slowly. As it opened wider the head of a white horse appeared, and at that very moment a bell rang through the house.

The lights turned higher, and the horse's head backed

away. The bell was insistent, and it was not until the hostess left the room that it was silenced.

Her voice was heard, as the horse's footsteps receded, saying, 'No, there has been no murder. No, there has been no murder.'

Titus left the room and found his way up to the nursery. To be alone was the only thing he wished. All through the night, at hourly intervals, a bell pealed through the house, and it would seem impossible that anyone could sleep in it, as they heard, 'No, there has been no murder – No, there has been no murder.'

When it was light, and in between the hourly bell, Titus got off his bed and left the house, making as little sound as possible. He left by the front door, and climbed up the steep steps that led from the Hidden House to the long drive. It took him some time to reach the road on which he had been waylaid only the day before.

'That is another end,' he thought. 'Let there be a new beginning.'

35

Search Without End

As Titus walked he decided that whatever happened he would never again be waylaid, and he hoped for his journey on the sea.

By the quiet of the road he judged that he was still on a sidetrack and he imagined that he would have to walk for some time before he reached a road that would lead him to a larger road that might take him seawards. The obscene man had said that he was walking seawards, and he clung to this, as to perhaps the only truth he might have uttered.

He walked onwards. His thoughts were of a future, which he could not see, but which he felt. The landscape changed slightly, from a rural emptiness to an occasional lonely house. At last he reached a crossroads with signposts. He could see that to continue straight ahead would lead nowhere, but to turn left into a wider, less arcane road might begin to lead to what he was seeking. Grass verge gave way to a path, then to a pavement, houses in ones and twos became rows of identical homes. Further on, his journey brought him to an old town built round a square. There was little life in it, but enough for him to feel that he might ask directions.

'The sea?' he asked of one old man. He put his hand to his ear, and Titus repeated the question. Taking his arm, the old man led him to a sign which indicated that there would be transport for such a purpose. A little group of people stood by the sign and he took his place with them. They waited patiently, until up rumbled a green vehicle, and from which people emerged with friendly greetings to those waiting.

Titus followed, and sat down on a seat. He had no idea where he was to go, but when asked he said 'To the end', which seemed to satisfy the conductor.

The vehicle stopped and started, disgorged and picked up people all along the road, sometimes taking in parcels, sometimes delivering them to people waiting at the roadside.

The landscape became more urban, then disappeared behind woods, and emerging from a cathedral of trees on to an open road he saw ahead of him the horizon, and the pale line of blue that separated the sky from the sea.

He was on his way. They went down a steep hill and reached what was presumably the edge of a big town, judging by the smoking chimneys and large areas of unattractive roofscapes. It had begun to rain and an unappetising smell of malt permeated the vehicle each time the door opened and closed. There were no trees, and the people walking briskly because of the rain had the worried look of animals trying to reach their respective lairs.

The green bus drew up at what must have been the 'end' of its journey, for everyone got up, collecting their bundles, and children, and making their way out.

The end of the road was a railway station. Titus followed the crowd. He spoke to a man at the gate.

'To the sea – to the boats?' he asked.

The man looked at a large clock above them and said, 'You're lucky. One'll be going in a quarter-hour. Have you got your ticket? Get it there.'

A train came slowly along the platform and Titus got in. It stopped and started, and went slowly along, past cranes and sidings until it left the town, and on its left was the sea. They travelled more and more slowly, until more cranes came into sight, then boats of many sizes and for many purposes, until the train stopped, and Titus saw it could go no further.

As he got down and walked along the grey platform, he knew that at last he was determining for once his own life.

He asked a man moving long cardboard boxes of flowers what boats there were and where they were going, and if he could get a passage.

'Well, there's the night boat – you're in luck. It only goes three times a week from here. You won't find no trouble getting on it. Look, I'm going that way. Come with me.'

They walked along the platform, and past a huge empty shed with wooden tables, emerging on to a quay, with a two-funnelled boat waiting. There was a gangplank, and people leaning on the rails of the boat, watching as others made their way up.

Titus's spirit was full of anticipation for a course of life that he alone had decided upon. Hitherto events had happened because he had not cared enough to avoid them. There was a tight knot of apprehension in him, no fear. He had made a deliberate decision and fate, somewhere, had helped him. He found himself on the boat, and he walked around the deck and watched the crane loading their cargo into the hold.

There was a friendliness among the people, both those who were travelling and the crew. It was cold, the rain had stopped, but the wind was rising, and jokes were interchanged as to the likelihood of a stormy crossing.

It took a little time for Titus to realise that the cranes

had finished loading and that the engines were throbbing, and although he was cold, for his clothing was
scanty, he wanted to see the vessel edging its way out
of the harbour and into the open sea. The gulls with
their greedy screeching flapped and swooped on to
the debris that was thrown overboard, and he stood
watching and listening, and although he had no physical
or emotional impediments to discard, he felt as though
he too could throw into the sea the dross he had
gathered over the last few years, and learn to hope
again.

The cold became too intense as the wind rose, and
the boat began to roll. He would have preferred to remain
on deck, but his feet and hands were numb. He made
his way down some steps and found an empty seat.
Someone nearby noticed how cold he seemed and
brought a rug to cover him. It took some time for him
to warm up and longer still to sleep.

Titus was awoken by the activity around him and the
voices that had the excited ring of people arriving, so
he knew that he was nearing the end of this particular
journey.

He rubbed his eyes and massaged his face, and he was
fully awake. He had no luggage to collect, but one rug
to return to its owner. He went up the steps to the deck
and made his way to the bows of the vessel. The roll of

the ship had ceased and the throbbing of the engines had diminished.

The morning mist was tangible in its grey whiteness. As the ship slowed he saw through the film faint forms which took the shape of enormous sea animals – each one an island, each alone, each wrapped in its own silent, private world. There was an aura of something he knew: something from the past; something that surrounded his whole being. Was it a caul or a shroud?

The ship moved slowly into harbour. The noise and bustle of disembarking prevented his introspection. He stepped on to firm ground and saw in front of him a quay, with its paraphernalia of cranes, and boats, and lobster pots.

The town behind was misty. Houses grew out of the rock and faced the sea, as though it was one element with the land and sky.

There was a sense of welcome in the faces of the weather-beaten men on shore and one man, seeing the hesitation in Titus, asked him, 'You staying or going on?'

'Well, I'm not sure . . . quite. Where else is there to go?'

'Well, there's a boat over in an hour to the little island – they only go three times a week now. Have you any luggage?'

'No, I haven't – I came without any.'

'Well, that's easy enough, then. You can get some breakfast and catch it then. You can get your ticket on the boat – just over there. She's in already.'

He pointed to a small boat that was being loaded, across the other side of the harbour.

Titus had breakfast and returned to the boat that had been pointed out to him. He went on board. There were a few people already there. It moved slightly as the waves lapped the harbour wall. He had a feeling of both emptiness and elation in the pit of his stomach. He stood alone. He waited. Time was slow. If asked, he could not explain the turmoil within him but he felt as though all that he was and had become was on the verge of anni-hilation, ready to embrace an event that was bigger than himself. A sense of the power of life elated him, but he presented to the outside world the figure of a man standing alone and serene.

The time came for the small ship to cast anchor and move slowly out of its harbour.

There was still a sea mist, and as the boat sailed out he heard the gulls and the shouts of men in the distance. The sound of foghorns added to the mystery of what lay beyond.

The sea was calm. He was alone. The mist lifted, and to his right a school of dolphins appeared and disappeared. The boat sailed between two small islands, dotted with black birds – 'cormorants' he heard someone say.

And then again, ahead lay a smaller island than those they had just negotiated. It was in the shape of a dolphin, with a little break between it and its progeny, but inextricably joined.

The boat approached the island. They could see the inlets and caves and rocks, and the seabirds whose home it was.

A jetty appeared, dotted with figures sitting on the sea wall. Hands and handkerchiefs were raised, and as they drew nearer the figures on the jetty became clearer. There were the shapes of horses and again the sound of gulls. An unaccountable nostalgia overwhelmed Titus.

The narrow entrance to the jetty was difficult, but slowly the boat turned and came to rest alongside the narrow quay.

There was a stillness and a silence within him. He hardly dared raise his eyes, and when he did his stomach turned and he knew that his journey was not an end but a beginning.

Among those watching the arrival of the boat from the jetty wall was the man whose eyes and very being had haunted Titus since he had first seen him.

By his side was a small girl, excited at all the fun of

activity. Dogs chased each other joyfully. To them, life was for living, and as Titus watched this man, whom he knew, as himself, the same virtue displayed itself. Life and the love of it were paramount. There was no longer any tragic groping. What he understood was a lust for life. The excitement of life transmitted itself into the little girl, and to two young boys, who joined the group.

They left the wall, and watched as suitcases, provisions and all the sundry necessities of island life were unloaded. The man, tall, dark, urgent, hoisted the little girl on his back.

Titus had reached an anchorage. He knew that his past and his future, his whole being, his reason, were here.

As he began to walk away from the jetty, through the small tunnel hacked out of the rock, he was joined by the man and his children. Together they made their way up the steep hill. Titus no longer felt alone, but a part of someone who would shape his life to come. There's not a road, not a track, but it will lead him home.